"I'm Adam Blessing," I said. My first name really was Adam. My mother's name had been Annabell Blessing. I doubt that anyone in the town of Storm remembered who she married, but I was playing it safe by dropping my father's name altogether.

"I know your name," this girl said.

"That's the thing about a small town," I said.

"What is?"

"Everyone knows everyone else's business," I said.

"You know I'm buying a depilatory for my hairy legs," she said, "and all I know is your name. Is that fair, even or equal?"

I laughed. I like funny girls. I always have.

"Sensitive characters, snappy dialogue—a sure draw."   —*School Library Journal*

THE SON
OF SOMEONE
FAMOUS

BOOKS BY M. E. KERR

Dinky Hocker Shoots Smack!
Best of the Best Books (YA) 1970–83 (ALA)
Best Children's Books of 1972, *School Library Journal*
ALA Notable Children's Books of 1972

If I Love You, Am I Trapped Forever?
Honor Book, *Book World* Children's Spring Book Festival, 1973
Outstanding Children's Books of 1973, *The New York Times*

The Son of Someone Famous
(AN URSULA NORDSTROM BOOK)
Best Children's Books of 1974, *School Library Journal*
"Best of the Best" Children's Books 1966–1978, *School Library Journal*

Is That You, Miss Blue?
(AN URSULA NORDSTROM BOOK)
Outstanding Children's Books of 1975, *The New York Times*
ALA Notable Children's Books of 1975
Best Books for Young Adults, 1975 (ALA)

Love Is a Missing Person
(AN URSULA NORDSTROM BOOK)

I'll Love You When You're More Like Me
(AN URSULA NORDSTROM BOOK)
Best Children's Books of 1977, *School Library Journal*

Gentlehands
(AN URSULA NORDSTROM BOOK)
Best Books for Young Adults, 1978 (ALA)
ALA Notable Children's Books of 1978
Best Children's Books of 1978, *School Library Journal*
Winner, 1978 Christopher Award
Best Children's Books of 1978, *The New York Times*

THE SON OF SOMEONE FAMOUS

M. E. KERR

An Ursula Nordstrom Book

HarperKeypoint
An Imprint of HarperCollinsPublishers

The lines on page 142 are taken from "To a Fat Lady Seen from a Train" by Frances Cornford from COLLECTED POEMS by Frances Cornford, copyright 1954 by Dufour Editions. Reprinted by permission of Dufour Editions, Inc., Cresset Press, and Barrie & Jenkins. The lines on page 165 are taken from "The New Mistress" from "A Shropshire Lad"—Authorised Edition—from THE COLLECTED POEMS OF A. E. HOUSMAN. Copyright 1939, 1940, © 1965 by Holt, Rinehart and Winston Inc. Copyright © 1967, 1968 by Robert E. Symons. Reprinted by permission of Holt, Rinehart and Winston Inc. Also reprinted by permission of The Society of Authors as the literary representatives of the Estate of A. E. Housman; and by Jonathan Cape Ltd., publisher of A. E. Housman's COLLECTED POEMS.

THE SON OF SOMEONE FAMOUS

LC Number 73-14338
ISBN 0-06-023146-7
ISBN 0-06-023147-5 (lib. bdg.)
ISBN 0-06-447069-5 (pbk.)
Harper Keypoint is an imprint of Harper Trophy,
a division of HarperCollins Publishers.
First Harper Keypoint edition, 1991.

For Barbara Dicks

Notes for a Novel by B.B.B.

This story begins the winter I thought I was turning into a boy. It isn't a story about that, though; I'm still a girl. It's the story of the son of someone famous. You'd know the name instantly. You may even guess it before I'm finished. But I'm not going to tell you outright. If I did, I'd have to leave out a lot so that I wouldn't be sued. I don't intend to leave out anything. Therefore I'm going to call the boy Adam Blessing, which was what he called himself when he came to live with Charlie Blessing, his grandfather.

Adam came to Storm, Vermont, during one of those freezing weeks before Christmas, when I was trying to figure out some way to vanish from the face of the earth forever. That winter, the two things I thought about most were a) ending it all, and b) running

1

away to New York City, where no one knew me, or cared that my name was Brenda Belle Blossom and that I was growing a small fringe of hair above my upper lip. My voice was deepening, too. I am almost sure that was the winter certain telephone operators first began answering me, "Yes, sir," and "Just one moment, sir, while I look up the number."

Adam Blessing looked like any other average sixteen-year-old boy: red hair, freckles, green eyes—neither handsome nor homely. If I had known then who he really was, I probably would have seen his famous father in his face. I know that now every time I see a photograph of his father, or see his father on television, I see Adam, even though Adam never spoke with that much confidence or looked that sure of himself.

All anyone really knew about Adam was that he was one of Charlie's grandsons, and that he had come to live with Charlie. As my Aunt Faith said when she heard the news, "Heaven help that poor kid."

I was just fifteen that winter. I was the town tomboy, fatherless, flat-chested, and an only child. The only thing I did well was grow things. I had, and maybe still have, the greenest thumb in Burlington County. I can grow anything, even orchids if I put my mind to it, but what I love to grow most is garbage: avocado pits, pineapple tops, grapefruit seeds, sweet potatoes that have gone soft—things that are usually thrown out.

2

My mother and my Aunt Faith and I live in the white house at the very top of Maple Hill. From my bedroom window I can look down on Charlie Blessing's bunglow at the bottom of the hill, on Ski Tow Avenue.

Sometimes in the middle of the night I'd have a dream that my father wasn't dead. He'd appear in my room looking as handsome as he does in his photographs, and he'd hold out his hand and tell me he was taking me back to Omaha with him. (He was born and raised in Omaha, Nebraska.) I'd be all smiles, all set to go with him, and then he'd keep repeating Oma-ha-ha, Oma-ha-ha-ha, Oma-ha-ha-ha-ha-ha, until all that was left was the sound of laughter. I'd wake up angry and hurt, because the joke was on me. He wasn't alive and I wasn't going anyplace.

Sometimes after that dream I'd get up and go to the bathroom. I always felt very lonely after that dream. I'd stare out the window, and at those times I'd always be grateful for Charlie Blessing's lights. They were on, no matter the time of night. My Aunt Faith said it was because Charlie drank. She never said Charlie drank quite a bit, or Charlie sometimes got drunk; she said flatly: "Charlie drinks." She said, "Charlie drinks by himself, which is the worst kind of drinking. It means he's brooding. It means he's bitter."

The fact that you almost never saw Charlie drinking in public did not mean that you never saw Charlie drunk in public. My aunt said Charlie couldn't afford to drink in public. But we've all seen him under the influence more times than we can count on our fingers. I think that's the reason I call him "Charlie" instead of Dr. Blessing, and it's probably the reason my mother and my aunt let me get away with it. He's the only adult in Storm I call by his first name.

Charlie wasn't an M.D.; he was a veterinarian. He was supposed to have been the best vet in the state of Vermont at one time. Christine Cutler's father was his assistant in those days. Then Charlie's only daughter, Annabell, was killed in an automobile accident, and Dr. Cutler began to run the Storm Animal Shelter single-handed. People began to prefer Dr. Cutler, and by the time Charlie was over his grief, no one wanted to bring sick pets to him. Eventually Dr. Cutler bought Charlie out. That was all years ago, before Charlie became a drinker, but there are still bad feelings between Dr. Cutler and Charlie.

The first day that I ever met Adam Blessing was a Wednesday in the late afternoon. In Storm, the after-school hangout is Corps Drugs on Central Avenue. From 3:30 until 5:00 p.m., it's packed. Around 5:30, it's dead.

That afternoon I was waiting for it to be dead. I was about to buy something called Hairgo from Mr. Corps. It was for my upper lip. I didn't want the kids around when I asked for it. I particularly didn't want

Christine Cutler anywhere within earshot, since I had an idea she already thought of me as a freak of some kind. I had a small reputation as something of a comedian, but not around Christine Cutler ever. I had this crush on her, which would be enough to make anyone want to puke, but the winter I thought I was turning into a boy, my crush on C.C. made me really begin to detest myself. I had decided there was probably something grossly wrong with me, and as a result I had developed a little hunched-over walk, as though I'd be less conspicuous instead of really kinky going around that way. I also used to never take off my coat. I also used to stand behind people a lot.

There I was, for a good part of that Wednesday afternoon, standing in Corps Drugs with my coat on, hidden by Marlon Fredenberg, the football captain, holding my right hand over my upper lip, pretending to be having another really swell afternoon with the gang at the old after-school hangout. I don't have to describe Christine Cutler to you; there is a Christine Cutler in every town. It wouldn't be enough to say she was blonde and blue-eyed. The Christine Cutlers of the world can have any color hair or eyes—they are still all alike. If you had to choose only one word to describe them, it would be Special. They are The Most Beautiful, The Most Popular, The Most Likely To Succeed; they are It.

That afternoon, Christine Cutler was holding

court, as usual, in the front booth. Everyone was flocked around her, hanging on her every word, practically drooling. I was drooping around over by the jukebox, clock-watching. 3:30, 4:15, 4:31. . . . Finally at 5:25, Ty Hardin, Christine Cutler's steady, stood up, took Her Majesty's coat from the hook and helped her into it. (Ty Hardin is the male It in *Storm*.) As soon as they left, the place cleared out so that you could have rolled a cannon through it.

"*What* is it you want?" Mr. Corps said. "Say that again."

"Hairgo," I said.

"Hairdo?" he said.

"*Go*," I said. "*Go*."

"What is it?" he said.

"It is something to make hair *go*," I said.

"Go where? Go back on your head? A hair net?"

"Mr. Corps," I said, "it is a depilatory."

At that moment I saw Adam Blessing.

He was sitting by himself in the very last booth, in the back of the store. He was writing in a notebook, but he stopped writing and looked up. Our eyes met, while Mr. Corps said to me, "Did you say you wanted a depilatory?"

"Yes, I said that was what I wanted," I answered. "I have a great deal of unsightly hair to remove from the soles of my feet."

I faced away from Adam because I knew that he was listening.

6

"You have hair on the soles of your feet?" Mr. Corps said.

My face felt hot and red, and my stomach was knotting up in panic, but my mouth went right on with the act. As far as my mouth is concerned when it comes to an embarrassing situation, there is no business like show business.

I can't even remember my next wisecrack . . . but that was the first day I ever spoke to Adam. That was A-Day.

From the Journal of A.

"You have hair on the soles of your feet?" the druggist said.

"Doesn't everyone?" this girl said.

"I don't," the druggist said. "I don't know anyone who does."

"Do you have to know someone who does to sell Hairgo?"

"No," the druggist said. "Just a moment and I'll see if I carry it."

There was something really dizzy about her. I mean that in a nice way. She had this way of scrunching up her shoulders which made it look like she was hiding inside her parka. She kept glancing back at me, and she was blushing—I guess because she'd asked for a depilatory before she knew there was someone else in the store. (She should only have known how often I used to help Billie Kay, my ex-stepmother, remove the hair from her upper arms.)

What I liked most about her was her voice. It was this low, husky voice. It was the way Billie Kay's voice sounded over the telephone if you called her when she was just waking up in the morning. In fact, it was the way Billie Kay's voice had sounded just a week before that Wednesday, when I called her around noon to give her the latest bad news about yours truly. "Oh, no, honey," she had said sadly in that throaty tone. "No, baby. They made a mistake, didn't they? You wouldn't do a thing like that."

This girl in the drugstore had black hair and brown eyes, my favorite combination . . . and she was very skinny, though I couldn't tell that on that first afternoon, since her body was camouflaged by her coat.

Before I'd overheard her conversation with the druggist, I'd been writing down my impressions of one Christine Cutler. She was the kind of girl I'd always been attracted to. She could have been enrolled at Miss Porter's School, at the Spence School, Miss Hewitt's, any one of those schools that turns out a certain kind of self-assured girl who knows what to wear and say, how to toss back her hair and look slightly bored, how to meet your eye and make you look away first—there is a certain privileged air about her. I had never had trouble getting a date with such a girl, once they knew who my father was, but I had always had difficulty maintaining the relationship once they discovered I was certainly not exactly a chip off the old block. Far from it.

The girl in the drugstore buying the depilatory was not that sort, so I wasn't afraid of her or in awe of her. The druggist was back in the Prescription Department for quite some time, and I finally spoke up, because the silence was too heavy.

I said, "I thought most people with hair on the soles of their feet were born without bones and only lived five hours."

She was very good at keeping a straight face. She said, "Who said *I* have bones? Who said *I* was alive?"

"I'm Adam Blessing," I said. My first name really was Adam. My mother's name had been Annabell Blessing. I doubt that anyone in the town of Storm remembered who she married, but I was playing it safe by dropping my father's name altogether.

"I know your name," this girl said.

"That's the thing about a small town," I said.

"What is?"

"Everyone knows everyone else's business," I said.

"You know I'm buying a depilatory for my hairy legs," she said, "and all I know is your name. Is that fair, even or equal?"

I laughed. I like funny girls. I always have. I sit

10

beside most girls without being able to think of anything to say but what my father would classify under the heading "manifest knowledge."

"A.J.," my father likes to instruct me, "never discuss manifest knowledge. Never comment on the weather, or the news of the day, or anything generally known, obvious and unnecessary to mention. If you can't be original, be silent."

Usually I am silent around girls. Billie Kay was a rare exception, but she was not a girl, she was a woman, and she was hilarious. . . . Maybe too hilarious for her own good. My father said he wanted a wife, not a performer. That was *one* of his excuses for ditching Billie Kay, anyway. Billie Kay's version of their breakup was that my father would never love a woman because my mother's death had made him too guilty. That was probably true. In his cups, my father often said, "I should have loved your mother more. She loved me with a passion, A.J.—an unbelievable passion."

I smiled at this girl in the drugstore and said, "Life isn't fair, or even, or equal, but I'll pretend it is and give you one of *my* secrets."

"I'm waiting," she said.

I put away my journal and walked toward her. "You have to remember, it really is a secret," I said.

She said, "So is the fact I have hairy legs."

"A lot of girls do," I said.

"But this is the first time I've ever bought anything to remove it," she said.

"My secret is a first, too."

"What is it?" she said.

"I was expelled from school," I told her, not even knowing why I was telling her. I hadn't planned to ever tell anyone in that town. "Usually I'm just suspended, or asked not to come back the next year. This time I was shipped out in midterm—pfffft, *fini!*"

"Was it a private school?" she asked.

"Yes. Choate."

"Never heard of it."

I shrugged, even though I was a little disappointed that she'd never heard of Choate. "Well, I can't impress you then."

"Is it a fancy school?"

"Most people think so."

"Why did you get expelled?"

"For cheating on an English exam," I told her.

"You really cheated?"

"Yes. I really cheated," I said. "But the thing is, I knew the poem by heart. I just blocked during the exam. I copied from the guy in front of me. But I really knew the poem. I still do. I can recite it right now."

At that point the druggist appeared carrying a small green tube and reading the print on it. "Remove facial hair with soft cream care," he recited. "Hair-go."

12

It was obvious the hair she wanted to remove was no more on her legs than on the soles of her feet. I hadn't noticed a mustache on her face. I used to help Billie Kay remove hers when she was doing her upper arms. Perhaps I'd spent too much time with an older woman who treated me like her buddy instead of her stepson; all I knew was it didn't faze me one way or the other when the druggist mentioned facial hair. But it fazed the girl plenty. She clapped her right hand across her mouth and mumbled something to the druggist.

"What?" the druggist said.

"I said I'll take it."

"Are you sure your mother knows you're fooling with this stuff?" the druggist said. For some reason he shot me a dirty look, and then continued, "It's one thing to take it off your legs, Brenda Belle, but you shouldn't play with something that can get into your eyes and blind you for life!"

Brenda Belle.

That was an unlikely name for her. That was a name for some bovine blonde with a sweet disposition and nothing to say.

"I'll walk you home and recite the poem," I horned in.

She still kept her hand across her mouth. "No!" she snapped back in a muffled exclamation.

"Why?" I asked.

"Stand aside, boy," the druggist commanded.

I stood aside while she passed him three dollars.

"You tell your mother what you bought before you use it," the druggist said.

"Skip the poem," I said to her. "I'll just walk you home."

She had two cents change coming, but she didn't wait for it. She headed out the door like the place was on fire.

"Hey, Brenda, wait!" I shouted, but she was out of sight before I could even get my coat from the hook.

The druggist eyed me coldly while I buttoned up and put my scarf around my neck. "What's the matter with a boy like you?" he said. "A boy like you ought to use his head. That was a highly personal transaction. A gentleman steps aside in such a circumstance, in case you didn't know!"

I didn't know how to answer him, how to get across that it hadn't seemed that highly personal because of knowing Billie Kay so well, all her beauty secrets and what she called "tricks of the trade."

I didn't have to answer, because he went right on bawling me out. "Now, you're a newcomer," he said, "and I don't know where you come from, but you learn yourself some manners, Mister, or don't show your face around my place!"

I was ashamed and then angry. There was a time when I'd have answered, "I don't think you know who I am!" and then told him. . . . But all that was in the past.

I was on my own, in Storm, Vermont, for the first time in my life. It was my own idea, because I was fresh out of ideas for my future. I wouldn't have blamed my father for completely disowning me at that point in my life. I was certainly nothing he could brag about, and everything that could disappoint him.

"The goddam trouble is," I told him over the long-distance phone one week before that Wednesday, "I'm sick of being the famous man's son!" (I knew I was copping out when I said it, but I said it anyway.)

"That's not the goddam trouble," he barked back. "That's the goddam excuse." You don't fool a man like my father. What I wished I could say was something like: I'm sorry I'm a lousy son, and I don't blame you if you hate me. I could never say anything like that to him. I thought that was probably part of the problem: I could never seem to level with him.

"Listen," I said. (I prefaced a lot of my sentences with "Listen" when I spoke to him; I guess it was because I was always so aware that he was forced to stop really important things to tend to my little messes.) "Listen, Dad, how about letting me go somewhere where no one knows who I am?"

"And where would *that* be?" he barked back at me.

"Couldn't I go live with Grandpa Blessing?"

There was a long silence. For a moment, I had this

15

crazy idea that my father was going to answer, *A.J.,
I want you with me.* It was really an insane thought,
not only because my father travels so much, but also
because how the hell would he explain me? I mean,
was a man like my father supposed to introduce me
by saying, "This is my son, the troublemaker. No
school will keep him. I have him with me because
there's no place else for him to go."

During that silence, I was also thinking of a line
from a Robert Frost poem: "Home is the place where,
when you have to go there, They have to take you in."

My father finally spoke. "Grandpa Blessing doesn't
even know you."

"He sends me a Christmas card every year. He
asks me to visit him. He says he lives all alone."

"Maybe he could use a little extra money," my
father said.

I said, "What?" I'd heard him very clearly, though;
I sometimes say "What?" when I'm in shock. The
idea of paying someone to take me in was what
shocked me. It shouldn't have, I guess. After all, my
father had paid Choate and all the other schools—
why not a relative?

My father said, "I said maybe we can work something out with him. Maybe that's not a bad idea."

So there I was, one week to the day later, on my
own, with this hick druggist dressing me down for
something I wasn't even sure I'd been that wrong
in doing.

16

"I'm very sorry, sir," I told the druggist as I picked up my books from the table. "You're absolutely right."

I was just going to have to learn . . . and to un-learn. . . . But I worried over how the girl felt about me, how Brenda Belle felt.

Oh, and incidentally, my grandfather refused my father's offer of money. He also told my father that I wouldn't need much of an allowance in Storm, either. No more than five dollars a week.

At Choate I'd been managing on one hundred and fifty a month.

Notes for a Novel by B.B.B.

Hairgo is a waxy substance you apply warm, let dry on your skin, and then rip off in exactly ten minutes. Seven minutes had passed that night when my mother entered my bedroom and said, "Always the clown, hmmm, Brenda Belle?"

What made her say that was the wax mustache I had made from Hairgo. It was colored pink and firmly attached to my upper lip.

I made a face and bowed low, letting her think I was just fooling around. I didn't want her to know my mustache was a depilatory, for fear she'd go into one of her famous panics.

"You know, Brenda Belle," she said, sitting down on the edge of my bed, "playing the clown isn't a very feminine thing to do. A funny woman is rarely a lady. I'm telling you this for your own good."

"You're probably right," I said, watching the second hand on my alarm clock. I had two minutes to go before it was time to remove the wax.

"I don't want to criticize you," my mother continued, "but it is a fact that very few female comediennes have happy lives."

"I don't particularly want to be a female comedienne," I said.

"Men laugh at funny women," my mother said, "but they rarely fall in love with them. A man likes a serious woman, a quiet woman."

"I plan to be a quiet, serious woman," I told her. "I promise."

"You don't seem to be headed in that direction, Brenda Belle. Even now you're intent on being the funny girl."

"I'm just practicing for a part in a school play," I said.

"Brenda Belle, you're not going to take a male role in a play, are you?"

"No," I said. "I've decided against it."

My fingers were playing with the wax mustache; I was seeing if it was possible to just pull it off in front of her, without her guessing its real purpose. The wax would not give an inch.

The ten minutes were up.

"You're at an age now when you should begin to

19

grow out of your tomboy stage," my mother said.

"I intend to," I said. "Excuse me, I have to go to the bathroom."

"Just a moment, Brenda Belle," she said.

"What is it?" I said impatiently.

"Please sit down, dear. I came to have a little . . . to discuss certain . . . to explain—" her voice drifted away without finishing.

I suddenly realized what she was up to. It was a rotten time for it. "I know the facts of life," I blurted out, and I could tell by the look in her eyes that she was hurt because I wouldn't sit down.

She stood up. "I guess you don't have time for a talk with your mother."

"Yes, I do," I said. "I just want to go to the bathroom first."

"I come in here for a serious talk with you, and you sit here wearing that mustache. Then you jump up and announce you know it all. I can see you're not in a receptive frame of mind."

"Just let me go to the bathroom first," I said desperately.

"Never mind," she answered, walking toward the door. "You'd rather be a clown and a know-it-all. I can see that."

I think she was really relieved that she didn't have to go through with it. She was hurt, too, but more relieved than hurt, because sex was number one on the list of the ten things she least liked discussing. My father was a close second.

I felt sorry for her, and sorry for myself, because there was nothing I could do then and there to make things better. I made a dive for the bathroom, and she went downstairs wearing that particular expression which I'd seen over and over that seemed to indicate I was her major cross to bear, if not the only one.

If you've ever ripped away a scab before it was completely healed, you know the feeling I had when I removed the wax mustache. The manufacturers of Hairgo weren't kidding when they advised the user to remove the wax in exactly ten minutes. Along with the wax, I removed a good deal of the skin above my upper lip. There was no blood, but there was a bright red tender bruise in the exact shape of a mustache.

For about an hour I rubbed the wound with vaseline, but nothing did any good. I was sitting on my bed, thinking of suicide and New York City again, when the telephone rang. It rang twice before my mother called up the stairs, "Brenda Belle, get that, will you? Faith and I are watching a movie."

That may have been true, but my mother was not all that engrossed in the movie, because I heard the little click meaning she was on the line shortly after I said hello.

"It's Adam," he said. "Remember me?"

"Yes," I said, and I tried to think of something funny to add, but I couldn't, not just because I was miserable, but also because I was practically dumbfounded to think he'd call me. I wondered if he wanted to make fun of me, and I was afraid, too, knowing my mother was listening and he might mention the depilatory.

"How are you?" he said.

"Fine," I answered.

"You're not mad or anything?"

"No."

"You sound different."

"It's hard to talk."

"Why?" he said.

"I'm in the midst of something."

"Oh . . . I'm sorry."

"That's all right."

"I was just going to ask you if you wanted to go to a movie or something Saturday night."

"Saturday night?" I said, picturing the scab I'd have over my upper lip by then. "*This* Saturday night?"

"Yes, this Saturday night."

"I can't," I said.

"Are you sure you're not mad?"

"Of course I'm not."

"You sound different."

22

"I'm doing something," I said.

"Okay," he said.

"Okay?" I said.

"Good-bye, then," he said.

"Good-bye."

I pressed the receiver button down, then up, and heard the click from the downstairs phone.

Then I sneaked out into the hall and leaned over the bannister to hear the conversation below.

"Wait for the commercial," my Aunt Faith said. "This scene has that marvelous Billie Kay Case in it; remember her, Millie?"

I could see my mother standing by the television set, waiting for the commercial, so she could turn down the sound and tell my aunt about my telephone conversation.

"Billie Kay Case is a very sad woman," my mother said. "It depresses me to watch her."

"She's a scream, though. Look at her!"

"What did she think was going to happen when she married him?" my mother said. "She was at least twenty years older!"

"Just enjoy the movie, Millie, and forget her personal life."

"It didn't take long for him to dump her. Five fast years. I knew he would," my mother said. My mother is something of an authority on the personal lives of all celebrities past and present. Once a week at the beauty parlor she thumbs through all the movie magazines and gossip sheets.

"Maybe Billie Kay dumped *him*," my Aunt Faith said.

"Not on your life!" my mother said emphatically. "He ditched her. He's going around with every young thing from Washington to Hollywood. He escorted a nineteen-year-old to a White House dinner, which in my opinion is a scandal!"

"Billie Kay must be in her late fifties now," Aunt Faith said. "This movie was made in the fifties."

"He *used* her," my mother said, "and then he tossed her out when she began to show her age."

"She is funny, though—look, *look*!"

Then the commercial came on, and my mother turned down the sound.

"Faith," my mother said, "what boy in this town is named Adam? What boy Brenda Belle's age is named Adam? I can't think of one."

"I can," said my aunt. "It's the new boy. Charlie Blessing's grandson."

"His grandson by which child?" my mother asked.

"I don't know," my aunt said. "Charlie had three sons and then poor Annabell. I just know he's got one of his grandsons living with him."

"That grandson called here for Brenda Belle," my mother said. "He asked her out."

"He asked Brenda Belle out?"

"He did."

"Out on a date?"

"He did."

"He did?"

"Yes. But wait until you hear this: Brenda Belle refused."

"How odd," my aunt said. "The whole thing. Odd."

"Is he a nice boy?" my mother asked.

"I have no idea. I feel sorry for him, though, living down there with Charlie."

"I'm worried about Brenda Belle," my mother said.

"That isn't news," said my aunt.

"I think she's too busy playing the clown."

"Better that she's doing something happy than something sad, Millie."

"Clowns aren't happy," said my mother. "Boys don't like clowns."

"This Adam must, if he's asking her for a date."

"I wish I could question her about it," my mother said, "but then she'd know I listened to her phone conversation."

My aunt said, "Turn up the sound now, Millie. The picture's going on."

After my mother turned up the sound on the TV set, she headed for the stairs.

I ran back to my bedroom. I knew she was on her way up to try and see if she could get me to talk about Adam.

By the time she got to my room, I was ready for her. I'd tied a silk scarf across my mouth, covering my Hairgo wound.

"Reach for the sky, Pardner!" I said when she walked through the door. "This is a stickup."

From the Journal of A.

"She's probably been told to stay away from you because of me," Grandpa Blessing said about a week after the day I met Brenda Belle Blossom in Corps Drugs. "Her mother doesn't approve of me. Not many people do."

"Don't blame yourself for everything," I told him. "She hasn't even been in school. She's probably sick."

"It won't be easy for you in Storm," he said. "I'm not exactly a hero around here."

"I'm not exactly a hero, either," I said, "so we're even."

We'd just finished dinner and we were sitting in the living room watching the evening news on television. Grandpa Blessing was polishing off another beer. My father never drank beer because he

27

said it gave a man a big belly, but it hadn't done that to my grandfather. He was tall and lean with the weathered face of an old Maine fisherman. He had thick white hair he wore in a brush cut, and blue eyes the color of a summer sky. I really liked his looks, and the kind of clothes he wore: old plaid flannel shirts and corduroy pants and those heavy ankle-length boots he ordered from Sears. He smoked a pipe, and I liked that too. My father chain-smokes cigarettes. You sit across the room from my father for a long time and you get the feeling his insides are a tangle of strained nerves, but my grandfather always looked calm and ready to deal with whatever came down the runway. That's the great thing about being around someone who's lived a long time: Not much will surprise him anymore; he's ready for you and whatever's happened to you, and you can talk to him about it.

The only trouble with Grandpa Blessing was he didn't really appreciate himself; he had this feeling he hadn't amounted to much. Late at night when he was really bombed, he'd call up this radio talk show that originated in Boston. He called himself "Chuck From Vermont," because when he was a young man during World War I, his army buddies used to call him Chuck. He'd been a cook in that war—it was long before he studied to be a vet. He knew a lot about food and traditions involving food, and Late

28

Night Larry, the man who ran the show, treated him like a real authority.

"Well, it's Chuck From Vermont," Late Night Larry would say. "What nugget of knowledge can you pass on to our listeners this morning?"

"This concerns saltcellars," my grandfather might answer. "In the Middle Ages the saltcellar stood in the center of the table, and was the symbol that divided high rank from low rank. Noblemen and others of rank sat above the salt, and commoners sat below the salt."

"Chuck From Vermont, you are something!" Late Night Larry would enthuse. "You always give us food for thought—ha, ha—and we appreciate hearing from you. How's that book coming along; have you finished it?"

"I'm working on it," my grandfather would tell him.

My grandfather wasn't working on a book at all. He told me he just liked to kid Late Night Larry. I think there was more than that to it, though. It was sort of his way of being someone. If Late Night Larry suspected that my grandfather was in his cups, he never mentioned it. He treated my grandfather with respect, and I suppose that alone was worth the price of the calls to Boston, even though my grandfather didn't really have the money for long-distance telephoning. My grandfather kept track of the cost, spaced his calls, and saved up to make them. It was his one extravagance.

Sometimes my grandfather would fall asleep over his beer with his clothes on. I'd wake up the next morning to find him still slumped in the living room chair, and all the lights still burning. And I'd cover him with a blanket before I set off for school.

He was a great talker on every subject but my mother. Once he'd taken a picture from his wallet to show me, one of my mother and father bringing me home from the hospital after I was born. It was years old and he hadn't looked at it in a long time, I could tell, because it was taken with an old Polaroid camera and the snapshot had never been coated (the old Polaroid pictures were preserved with a coating you had to apply yourself). There we were, all right, all three of us, but our faces had faded away. . . . My grandfather didn't like to talk about my mother. Once he asked me what my father said about her, and I told him my father felt badly because she loved him more than he loved her. My grandfather's comment was simply, "She was very young, A.J. Just a kid, not much older than you."

That night while we were watching the news on television, I'd asked him what Brenda Belle Blossom's mother was like.

"She was real pretty once," he said, "but she's like a present that stayed gift wrapped. No one ever got to appreciate it, though I think Hank Blossom tried hard. He was her sister's beau before he met Millie. Everyone thought Hank would marry Faith. He came from Omaha, Nebraska, and he rode in the rodeo. He was handsome as sin, a rascal who'd rather laugh than eat, and Faith and Hank were always howling their lungs out over just anything. But Faith wasn't the pretty one of the sisters."

"So he married Millie."

"Yes. She set about trying to get him out of the rodeo and into a suit of clothes with his hair slicked down. He left her a couple of times. It was Faith who always tried to get them to patch it up, even though it was Faith who loved Hank better than I love beer. The last time Hank left Millie, Millie was pregnant with your friend Brenda Belle. Faith found out Hank was in a rodeo out in Missouri. She talked Millie into going to see him. The one thing Millie'd always refused to do was to see Hank ride."

"What happened then?" I said.

"What happened was Hank looked up and saw Millie sitting there beside Faith, and Hank fell off his horse. Millie told it that he was drinking and couldn't stay on the critter, but Faith told it that the shock of seeing Millie's angry face threw him."

"Was he hurt?" I asked.

"Mortally," my grandfather said. "The horse kicked him in the head."

31

"Then Brenda Belle never knew her father?"

"Nope."

"Did Faith ever marry?"

"Faith was married for a short time," my grandfather said. "She married old Doc Hendricks, used to be county coroner. He was a good man, a kind man, but he was old and he died, and Faith and Millie moved in together."

"Brenda Belle and I have something in common then," I said.

"What's that?"

"Well, I never knew my mother, either." I could see it made him uncomfortable to bring up the subject of my mother again, so I babbled on. "It's harder for a girl, I guess. I feel sorry for her living with those two old ladies."

"Don't let that be the only reason you want to see a girl," my grandfather told me. "When you pity someone, sometimes all it means is you wish someone would pity you."

I was thinking that one over while the news continued on television.

Suddenly the subject was dropped. The reason was what came across our television screen then. It was my father getting out of a helicopter on the White House lawn. The Vice-President was waiting to meet him.

"Your old man's put on weight," my grandfather

said. "I saw pictures when he was in Moscow and he was a lot thinner."

"Yeah," I answered, watching my father, all smiles, shaking hands with the Veep.

"I didn't know he was heading for Washington," my grandfather said.

"Neither did I," I said. "I thought he was still in Paris."

"Maybe you'll see him at Christmas after all," my grandfather said. "Maybe he'll be sending for you."

I said, "I doubt it."

"Oh well, he's a busy man," my grandfather said.

"I haven't been with him the last two Christmases anyway," I said. "I spent them with Billie Kay."

"Did you want to spend them with him?"

"No," I lied. "Christmas is a commercial holiday. All the original meaning has gone out of Christmas." I'd gotten that line from some preacher at chapel.

"I never liked the original meaning to begin with," Grandpa Blessing said. "We shouldn't celebrate the day someone is born, or the day someone dies. You can't help being born, or dying; everyone's born and everyone dies. We should celebrate accomplishments."

"I never thought of that," I said.

"I'd like to find out the day beer was invented," my grandfather said. "I'd celebrate that day, all right."

The White House scene was off the screen and

there was a story about a train wreck being tele-vised. My grandfather went into the kitchen for an-other beer. I sat there watching the train wreck without really seeing it. I was thinking about my father. I wondered what my father said to people like the President and the Vice-President. I wondered if he ever interrupted them by saying, "Hell, that's manifest knowledge, don't bore me with it," as he often said to me; or, "Don't mouth other people's opinions. Form your own!"

When the telephone rang, I made no effort to answer it. A lot of people in Storm pestered my grand-father by calling him up to recite the symptoms of their cats and dogs. That way they decided whether or not the symptoms were serious enough to warrant a visit to Dr. Cutler. My grandfather was always polite and helpful, but I think it hurt him a lot. He never blamed Cutler outright for anything; he never said Cutler had stolen his practice, though that was the rumor in Storm. Marlon Fredenberg had told me that much the first week I was there. All my grand-father ever said about Cutler was that he had his rea-sons for not wanting anything to do with Cutler, and that included talking about Cutler. Marlon Freden-berg said the least Cutler could have done was ask my grandfather to assist him, but Cutler just bought him out; that ended that.

"Phone's for you!" my grandfather called from the kitchen.

I went out to answer it, figuring that if it was my father asking me to guess where he was calling from, I'd just say, "I suppose you're at Buckingham Palace, or the Kremlin, or the White House," to sort of take the wind out of his sails. I don't know why I wanted to do that, particularly. I just did. I wasn't much of a loving son. I should have been glad he'd call me at all.

"A.J.? How would you like a visitor for Christmas?" It wasn't my father. It was Billie Kay calling from New York City.

"You mean you'd come here?" I said. I was really glad to hear her voice, but in a way I couldn't picture Billie Kay in Storm. She liked luxury too much. I couldn't see her in my grandfather's house.

"I'll stay at the hotel," she said. "Will you and your grandfather invite me for Christmas dinner?"

"Well, I don't know about that," I said. I knew Billie Kay would expect this gala feast; she was very big on holidays and celebrating. I didn't see how I could ask my grandfather to spend the money on a turkey and all the trimmings, and my own allowance was too small. Then too, I remembered my grandfather's last call to Late Night Larry. He'd told Late Night Larry Christmas wasn't even celebrated in the early days in New England, because it was a feast day of the Church of England, against which the Pilgrims and Puritans were in rebellion. In 1659 a law was passed imposing a fine on anyone celebrating Christmas. ("You don't say!" Late Night Larry had responded. My grandfather had said, "I do say! Thanksgiving was the important day! Not this phony Christmas!")

"Let me talk to my grandfather," I told Billie Kay. I put my hand over the mouthpiece so she wouldn't hear our conversation.

"It's Billie Kay," I said. "She wants to make a big deal over Christmas, but I'd just as soon tell her we don't go in for phony holidays."

"We don't go in for fancy holidays," my grandfather said, "but we'll cook up a meal she won't forget. Tell her to come, A.J."

"Are you sure?" I said.

"Is the Pope Catholic?" he said.

"Billie Kay," I said, "we'd love to have you."

"Great, A.J. I'm bringing Janice. I hope you don't have any dogs there?"

"You can bring Janice," I said. "I'll make a reservation at the hotel."

After I finished talking with her, my grandfather brought his beer into the living room and sat down opposite me. "So we're going to have two dinner guests, huh?" he said.

"Janice is just a Siamese cat," I said.

"You know, A.J.," he said, "Christmas wasn't even celebrated in the early days in New England."

"Is that right?" I said. I didn't want to tell him

that I'd been sitting right beside him when he'd gone into all that with Late Night Larry. I knew he'd blacked out, the same way Billie Kay sometimes did when she drank too much. I let him finish. Then I said, "I'm sorry I got you into this, Grandpa."

"What are you talking about?" he said. "Times change. It isn't 1659 anymore."

"But I know you never even liked the original meaning of Christmas," I said.

"The original meaning has gone out of Christmas," he answered. "You said that yourself just a short while ago. Where's your memory, A.J.? It can mean anything we want it to mean!"

I laughed. "It'll mean a lot of work for you."

"I like to cook," he said. "Remember, you're talking to Chuck From Vermont. . . . I'll tell you something else, A.J."

"What's that?"

"I think we ought to have a tree. I think we ought to fix this place up so it looks a little more like Christmas!"

"Do we have the money?" I asked.

"No, we don't have the money," he said.

"I could wire my father for some," I said.

"Not on your sweet little behind," my grandfather said. "I've got a turkey in the deep freeze."

"But we shouldn't buy a tree."

"We won't. And we won't cut one down for our

own selfish purposes, either. We'll make a tree from pine branches," my grandfather said. "And we'll decorate it ourselves."

"What'll we use for decorations?" I said.

"What do we have the most of around here, A.J.?"

I looked at him, puzzled.

"Beer cans, A.J.!" my grandfather laughed. "Empty beer cans!"

Christmas was a week away.

Notes for a Novel by B.B.B.

"Where have you been?" Adam asked me a few days before Christmas. "Have you been sick?"

I was standing by my locker, getting out of my parka. I grabbed my wool muffler and draped it across my face like a veil. "I was asked to join the sheik's harem," I said. My Hairgo scab was gradually disappearing, but it was still there. I had covered it with pancake makeup, but on very close inspection there was a thin scar mustache.

"Seriously," Adam smiled, "how come you missed school this past week?"

It was all thanks to Aunt Faith, who'd persuaded my mother that the humiliation of going to school in that condition would far outweigh any damage done by missing five days of classes. Reluctantly my mother wrote an excuse for me, declaring I had been

39

felled by flu. I studied my lessons daily in our sun parlor, nursing my wound with skin creams and making dozens of promises to my mother that I would never fool with a depilatory again.

"Go away," I told Adam as I kept my muffler across my face. "The sheik is a jealous lover. Even now his spies are observing me."

The only person observing me, besides Adam Blessing, was Christine Cutler. Her locker was a few doors from mine.

"Hi, Brenda Belle!" she called over. "How are you?"

Since when had she cared how I was?

"Okay," I answered.

Adam was still standing there.

I told him, "If you must communicate with me, do so by telephone this evening. I cannot risk the sheik's disapproval."

He laughed and sauntered away, calling over his shoulder, "I'll see you in Science."

Then Christine Cutler came up behind me and said, "Do you want to be my partner in Science?"

I kept my face turned from hers. "Why do I need a partner?"

"You've been absent," she said. "We're working on experiments for the principle of conservation of mass."

"I don't like to work as a team," I said. Any other

time I would have given my right arm to be her partner, but not in the condition I was in.

"We have to work as partners," she said. "How about it?"

"Okay," I said giving up. "O-kay." I took off my muffler and faced her.

She didn't blink an eye; she didn't notice anything different about my face.

"Don't forget," she said. "We're partners. See you after Homeroom."

I mumbled something back and purposely headed in the opposite direction, toward the drinking fountain. I heard about six male voices shout out, "Hey, Christine, wait for me!" and over my shoulder I saw them scrambling forward to walk with her.

I began to wonder why she was suddenly interested in me. All through Homeroom, I feared the worst. Was it possible that Christine Cutler sensed some dreadful change taking place in my body? Since she was never known to show any interest in females, was it possible she was picking up weird vibrations?

Our Science teacher was named Ella Early. She always made me uncomfortable because I sometimes thought I'd wind up exactly like her. She was the kind of person it didn't matter how old she was, she was old, if you know what I mean: She was never young. She never wore colors, just black. She always had chalk dust on her dresses, and she wore her hair back in a bun, and her face looked as if it would break if she ever smiled, which she never did. You just knew that no one had ever said to her, "Ella, I love you," and that no one ever waited for her to come, or cared if she wasn't there. She lived by herself in a room at Miss Jameson's boarding house, and noons she ate at a table by herself in the cafeteria. She was the type you could never imagine having a father or mother or sisters or brothers. She was cranky and mean, and she was the only teacher who never put up decorations in her classroom at Christmas time. There were lots of nicknames for her: "The Robot," "Ella Late Who Has No Fate" and "E.E., The Worker Bee."

She was an example of what can happen to a person who nobody cares about, and I could see myself ending up that way after my mother and my aunt disowned me for never marrying. I'd probably get a job teaching in New York City where nobody knew me, and when I wasn't in school, I'd wander around the streets of the city talking to myself like a crazy.

Ella Early instructed us to place copper and sulphur in a sealed test tube; then we were supposed to weigh the mixture. I was concentrating on the assignment when Christine Cutler said to me, "Adam Blessing is certainly trying to get your attention, Brenda Belle."

Every time I looked up, he was grinning at me across the room.

"I can't help that," I said.

"You're not like I thought you were," she said.

I blushed with apprehension and fear. I was afraid of what she would say next. ("Brenda Belle, have you had a sex change?")

"What did you think I was like, anyway?" I muttered as we heated the copper and sulphur.

"I didn't think you were very cool," Christine said.

"Am I?" I said, trying to raise my voice an octave.

"Yeah," she answered in her best breathless tone. She was busy tossing back her long yellow hair and watching Adam watch me. He just kept watching me that way, and it began to make me nervous. I figured that he'd probably never get it out of his head that he'd witnessed me buying the Hairgo. Christine was sort of smiling in his direction, smiling at him smiling at me, and I began to imagine that she knew about the Hairgo, too, that while I was absent they'd laughed about it together.

"We're supposed to weigh this stuff now," I said.

"You weigh it," she said.

"I thought we were partners," I said.

"We are. I'll record the weight."

"You can't record the weight while you're looking across the room," I said.

"He's different from Storm boys, isn't he?" she said.

"Is he?"

"Not just his clothes," she said.

"What about his clothes?"

"He wears really nice clothes," she said. "Expensive clothes."

"He does?" I said. His clothes didn't look all that special to me; in fact, I'd never noticed his clothes.

"He has a certain self-assurance," she said.

"Miss Early is watching us," I said.

After we'd recorded the weight, while we were waiting for Miss Early to tell us how to graph the results, Christine Cutler said, "What are you doing Christmas Eve, Brenda Belle?"

"I haven't made up my mind yet," I said.

"I'm having a small party," she said. "Why don't you ask Adam Blessing to come to it with you?"

"I didn't know I was invited."

"I'm inviting you now."

"I'll try to make it," I said. That was the understatement of the year. I had never been invited to the Cutlers'. I wondered if she'd been afraid to invite me because I might not be able to think of anyone to ask. Her crowd was always paired off. I supposed she thought Adam and I were a pair.

"Come about eight o'clock," she said.

"No talking about anything but the assignment!"

Ella Early said. "This isn't a social hour!"

After the bell rang, Adam was waiting for me just outside the door of Science class.

I decided that if Christine Cutler couldn't see anything wrong with my face, chances were that Adam Blessing wouldn't, either.

It was a wrong decision.

As I glanced up at him, full face, and smiled, he said, "Is that what that stuff did to your face? I was wondering why you were trying to hide it."

"Lower your voice, creep!" I said angrily.

"I'm sorry," he said.

"You're really stupid about some things," I said.

"I'm sorry," he repeated. "I didn't know you were sensitive about it."

"You've been going to all-boy schools too long," I said. I was close to tears, but I wasn't going to let him know that. I thought of Marilyn Pepper's pimples, Sue Ellen Chayka's broken nose, and Diane Wattley's bowlegs—anything I could think of to keep from feeling sorry for myself. I told Adam, "You're no great prize, you know. I was just asked to a Christmas Eve party on condition that I don't bring you." The words just came out.

He looked really surprised. "You were?"

"I was," I said.

"Whose party?"

"Never mind," I said, hating my own big mouth

45

for really fixing things for me that time.

He walked beside me silently for a while, and then he said, "I'm doing something Christmas Eve, anyway."

Fine, I thought to myself; at least I spared myself the humiliation of being turned down.

"I don't like parties, anyway," he said. "I've been to so many parties where people mouth other people's opinions that it all bores me. All you hear at parties is a lot of manifest knowledge."

"A lot of what?" I asked him.

"Manifest knowledge," he answered.

"I know it," I said. I had no idea what he was talking about. "Oh, that's the truth, all right," I said.

"I've got this friend coming in from New York City to spend Christmas with me," he said.

"Did he go to school with you?"

"It's a she," he said.

"Great!" I said, nearly bent double by a sudden stab of disappointment. "I hope you have a fabulous time."

"It's nothing like that," he said. "She's old enough to be my grandmother."

I would have to go to Christine Cutler's alone. It wasn't a place you took just anyone.

"I don't particularly like old people," I managed to carry on the conversation. "They meddle with your life."

46

"Not Billie Kay," he said. "She isn't a meddler."

"Oh, la-di-da," I said. "I gather you mean Billie Kay Case of Hollywood fame and fortune."

"How did you know?" he said.

"The movie star *I'm* spending Christmas Eve with told me," I said.

"But Billie Kay Case *is* who I mean," Adam said.

"We must all get together and drop names," I said.

"Honestly, Brenda Belle, she really is coming to see me."

"I'll roll out the carpet down Central Avenue," I said. "Do bring her into Corps for a Manhattan with an olive in it."

"You don't put olives in Manhattans," he said. "Olives go in Martinis."

"Keep your mouth shut about my upper lip," I said as we came to the end of the hall. "Don't spread it around."

"You can trust me," he said. "Have you told anyone I was expelled?"

"No."

"Brenda Belle, I don't know why I confide in you, but I do. I'd appreciate it if you'd keep it quiet about Billie Kay coming to Storm. She doesn't like a lot of bother now that she's getting older."

"Knock it off," I said.

"I mean it."

"A joke's a joke," I said, "but an all-day running joke is a bore. I can't be 'on' all the time. You'd better know that about me right now. Very few female comediennes have happy lives."

"Brenda Belle, listen to me," he said. "Billie Kay is really coming here. Please believe that."

"You may wear expensive clothes," I said, looking at his clothes and not seeing any difference from other people's clothes, "but you have big problems. You not only cheat, you lie."

I saw the look of disappointment on his face. "All of those things," he said, and then he walked away from me.

That was fine as far as I was concerned. I had enough *not* going for me, without having a sickie tailing me around. It was funny, because I'd really liked him up until that conversation. But after that conversation, I thought, No wonder he's interested in me—he's slightly crazy. Whacked out. He'd probably been expelled from that school because of trouble with his head, I decided.

What I was looking for at that point in my life was normal companionship, not a misfit. I wanted someone who fit, so I'd feel I fit, too.

After struggling all through Algebra with problems in polynomial multiplication, I bumped into Christine Cutler in the hall.

"Did you ask him?" she said.

"Yes," I said, "but he said he didn't want to come, because it'd just be a lot of people mouthing other people's opinions, which bores him. I'll be there, though . . . around eight-on-the-dot."

That night before supper, Christine Cutler called to say that she simply had to cut her party list down, that she was only having very close friends.

"You understand, don't you, Brenda Belle?"

"Absolutely," I said, "I understand."

I had the dream again, that night, about Omaha-ha-ha-ha-ha-ha.

From the Journal of A.

I'll never forget the Christmas my father's photograph was on the cover of *Time* magazine. It was during the early years of his marriage to Billie Kay. It had been a terrific year for my father. It had been the first year he'd ever been asked to the White House for dinner, and the year his photograph began appearing in newspapers and his name mentioned in gossip columns. We were trimming the tree, and my father was gulping down eggnog laced with brandy. When all the fancy decorations were tied to the tree's branches, my father said, "Now for the finishing touch." He took the photograph of himself on the cover of *Time* and pinned it to the very top of the tree. "There's our star!" he said. Then he fell over backward and knocked the tree down, and everything broke.

I was remembering that on Christmas Eve afternoon, while I helped my grandfather paint empty beer cans gold and silver.

My grandfather had an awful hangover. The night before he'd phoned Late Night Larry to tell him he'd found a publisher for his book. ("When you become famous, Chuck From Vermont, don't forget your friends in Radioland!").

"You look down in the dumps, A.J.," my grandfather said.

"I'm not, though," I answered him. I was down, I guess. I often was at Christmas. One of the reasons I was down that Christmas was because I'd found out who was giving the Christmas party Brenda Belle had mentioned—the one she'd been invited to, on condition she didn't bring me. It was Christine Cutler.

I was genuinely surprised. Maybe it had been my imagination, but I'd thought Christine Cutler took to me in some strange way. It was nothing I could put my finger on; it was a feeling I got sometimes when I'd see her in the hall or across a classroom. I'd thought there was just the slightest spark, no bells ringing or rockets going off, but the tiniest kind of undercurrent. I'd get her eye and she'd hold my eyes with hers, and I'd definitely feel this slight charge passing between us.

After Brenda Belle told me what she did, I crossed it off to wishful thinking on my part. Still, to tell someone she couldn't come if she brought me didn't do a lot for my ego. I wondered if it had something to do with the rift between my grandfather and Dr. Cutler. I wanted to blame it on that, but a part of me said to just face facts: The only time someone like Christine Cutler noticed yours truly was when she knew whose son I was. . . . In addition, Brenda Belle's attitude toward me had changed. I knew she took me for this stupid phony; I knew she thought I made up things like Billie Kay's coming so I could get attention.

I was beginning to feel like an outcast in Storm; I was beginning to wish they all knew who I really was.

"Doesn't anyone in this town remember my mother's marriage to my father?" I asked Grandpa Blessing.

He said, "First of all, no one knows you're Annabell's son, A.J. And secondly, no one remembers who she was married to. Your mother met your father in New York City. He wasn't anyone in those days. She died a year after she married him. It's all forgotten."

"I'm glad," I lied. I didn't want him to know how much trouble I was having making it on my own.

"If you're worried about anyone finding out who you are, stop worrying," he said. "I never mention your father's name around here. I hardly knew him, anyway, and I don't believe in reflected glory."

My grandfather was busy tying the painted cans to the tree we'd made.

He said, "Of course, I don't know how you're going to explain Billie Kay Case's visit. Someone might recognize her, never mind the phony name she's registering under down at the hotel. A lot of her old movies are showing on TV."

"If someone should recognize her," I said, "I'll just say she's a friend."

"Or a distant relative," he said. "After all, there's quite an age difference for her to be your friend. How old is she, A.J.?"

"I'm not supposed to say," I said. "She's fifty-eight. She doesn't look it, though."

"She's only nine years younger than I am," he said.

"She's had her face lifted."

"Why'd she do a fool thing like that?"

"She didn't want to look older than my father."

"Your father let her do that?" he said.

"By that time he was hardly ever home," I said. "He didn't know what we were doing."

My grandfather stepped back to look at his handiwork. I did, too. I had to smile. It was a crazy-looking tree we'd made—not beautiful, but unique and zany, with a certain brave and punchy spirit, like someone who'd come to a formal dinner party in the wrong clothes and turned out to be the life of the party.

"We did a good job, A.J.!" my grandfather said. "Now, that's a Christmas tree! We didn't destroy anything living to make it, and we didn't waste money to trim it. . . . Speaking of money, A.J.," he said, reaching into his trouser pocket, "I've managed to come up with a few dollars I completely forgot I had. How about you running out and buying that girl a gift? Corps Drugs is still open, and they've got gift boxes of candy or toilet water—I don't know why they put something to sell in a bottle and call it by that name—but here, A.J." He shoved the money at me.

"No," I said. "Save it for your telephone bill. I already bought Billie Kay a box of chocolate-covered cherries. She loves them."

"I don't mean Billie Kay. I mean the Blossom girl. You sort of take to her, don't you?"

"Not really," I said. "I think she takes after her mother. I think she's a gift-wrapped package no one can get to."

"She's not as pretty as her mother was," Grandpa Blessing said. "She shouldn't be playing that hard to get."

"Well what about me?" I said. "I'm no bargain, either."

"What makes you say a thing like that?"

"No one's exactly knocking themselves out over me," I said.

"Well," he said, "that may be my fault." He put the money back in his pocket and slumped down on the couch. "It's going to be harder being my grandson than being your father's son. Reflected glory is bad enough to live with, but reflected blame is worse."

"Blame for what?" I said. "What'd you ever do wrong?"

"I became the town drunk, for one thing," he said.

"I've seen my father drunk a lot of times."

"That's different, A.J. . . . If you get drunk now and then at a big party at the Waldorf Astoria in New York City, that's a way of life. If you get drunk in a little house all by yourself, that's a way out of life. I've been ducking out."

"That's your business," I said.

"Maybe this whole idea of you coming to live with me is a bad one," he said. "How're you ever going to make nice friends?"

"And that's *my* business," I said. "I'll learn."

I was glad the telephone rang then. We were both working our way into gloomy moods. It was almost time for me to meet Billie Kay's bus. Usually Billie Kay took a limousine from an airport to a town she was visiting, but she'd decided she'd be less conspicuous arriving in Storm by bus. No one expected to see an old movie star getting off a Greyhound.

My grandfather was in the kitchen talking to someone on the phone.

I heard him say, "Is he eating? Is his nose warm?"

More free advice, I thought, and then I thought of the Christmas Eve party at the Cutlers' . . . and of Christine Cutler telling Brenda Belle she could come on condition she didn't bring me.

For some reason, at that moment, I could picture Christine Cutler very clearly in my mind. I could see her blonde hair spilling to her shoulders, and I could remember how she moved down the hall at school. She had that way of walking that was almost a strut, and I wondered why I was suddenly able to recall quite a lot about her: the fact that she wore white most of the time, and the tiny gold bracelets that jingled at her wrist, and her voice, breathless-sounding and soft.

I remembered one time when my father was trying to get this new Hollywood starlet to go out with him. She wasn't even famous; he was so much more famous than anyone she probably knew. She didn't even seem surprised he'd called her. She didn't try to draw the conversation out, or explain why she wouldn't go on a date with him. She simply rejected him. I heard the whole thing. When he hung up, I waited for him to curse and make some sort of derogatory remark about her.

Instead, he said, "By God, I like her style!"

Then he sent her six dozen long-stemmed white roses.

At the time, I simply didn't understand it. Then this Psychology teacher we had at school enlightened me on the subject. He had his own name for it: the Groucho Marx syndrome. He called it that because there was a story about the comedian Groucho Marx. Groucho had been trying for years to get a membership in this fancy club, but the club kept refusing him. When the club finally relented and asked him to join, Groucho said he didn't want to belong to any club that would have him as a member.

In a way, my father was like that about women. He chased the ones who weren't interested. When one became interested, he lost his interest.

It was a form of masochism. Our Psych teacher said it was rooted in a deep inferiority complex. I'm not sure I bought that. My father was the last man you could imagine having an inferiority complex. He had everything going for him, and even if he did chase women who weren't interested at the start, it wasn't long before they did an about-face.

I *did* have an inferiority complex. To be frank about the whole matter, and I was being frank with myself that Christmas Eve afternoon, I was plain inferior. I was. I tried to compare myself with my father at my age. He'd been a brilliant student; he'd really sweated to get where he was. Nobody'd handed him anything, and he'd come from a real nothing family. . . . Then look at me—all I was, was the son of. I wasn't even a person in my own right. I couldn't even make it in a hick town like Storm.

I just hoped I wasn't going to turn into this masochist; I made a little promise to myself then and there that I wasn't. The hell with the Christine Cutlers of this world. If they didn't want the pleasure of knowing me, their loss, I told myself, *their loss!*

From the kitchen, I heard my grandfather say, "No, don't worm him! People should never worm their animals themselves. Take him to Dr. Cutler."

I sat there looking at the tree with the beer cans tied to it and listening to my grandfather. It was a funny thing, but I loved him a whole lot right at that moment. . . . Because no matter what life had done to him, he wasn't mean.

I didn't imagine life had many goodies in store for me, either, and I just hoped I'd make it through without being mean, too.

Because there were times when you could feel the meanness creeping into your own soul, times when you wanted to hurt someone, wanted someone to have a party where no one would show up . . . things like that.

Notes for a Novel by B.B.B.

Dear Christine,
This is a note to tell you I see through your dumb
Christmas Eve invitation, and I think you are a louse
for trying to use me. If you only knew what a neat
person I thought you were before you pulled this
on me. I thought about you a lot, honestly. Christine,
honestly, you were one person I wanted to trust be-
cause you were special to me. I guess you don't care
what I think of you, which is a shame because you
were maybe the only person I really—

"Brenda Belle," my mother said to me late Christmas Eve afternoon, "did you write this note?"

"What are you doing going through my wastebasket?" I said. "Living here is like being investigated by the FBI."

"I'm glad you decided not to finish it," my mother said. "You're getting to be a little old for this kind of schoolgirl crush."

"I don't have a crush on her," I lied.

"You've had a crush on her for some time. I wonder if you're aware how often you've brought up her name."

"Excuse me for living," I said.

"I'm not trying to humiliate you," my mother said, "but I do want you to think more about your femininity."

"What do you think I was thinking about when I ripped off half the skin on my face?" I told her.

"Femininity is inside, not outside," my mother said. It's a feeling one has about oneself, a feeling that one is a woman."

"One finds that difficult to believe when one is sprouting a mustache," I said.

"A little facial hair is normal, Brenda Belle."

"Tell that to the bearded lady in the circus."

"Brenda Belle," she said, sitting on the edge of my bed and folding her hands in her lap, "your Aunt Faith was very much like you when she was young. She was very busy being the smart aleck, slapping her knees when she laughed, getting to her feet in company to mimic someone—she just never thought very much about how she looked to the opposite sex. Our mother just let her develop into a boisterous type, heedless of how it would affect her relationships with men. . . . I'm afraid she missed out on the important things in life. She married too late, and old Doc Hendricks never gave her a child. I don't want that to happen to you, dear." My mother always said a man *gave* a woman a child, as though the woman had no part in its conception.

I felt like asking my mother about her own marriage to my father. I doubt very much that it would go down in history as one of the more successful undertakings between two people. My mother seldom spoke well of my father; she seldom spoke about him at all.

I said, "I'm not planning to imitate Aunt Faith."

"Whether you're *planning* it or not, you remind me of Faith at your age."

She tossed my note to Christine Cutler back into the wastebasket and said, "Christine Cutler is no one to look up to, believe me. I know things about her father that are repulsive and revolting."

"For instance?" I said.

"I don't intend to repeat them," she said, "but you can take my word . . . and blood will always tell."

"What does that mean, what does 'blood will always tell' mean?"

"It means that she's his daughter and she has some of him in her makeup," my mother said.

I said, "Oh, everyone knows he cheated Charlie

out of the business. That's old news."

"Everyone does not know everything," my mother said. "Now, tell me about Charlie's grandson."

"What about him?"

"He seems like a nice boy."

"You've never even met him, Mother."

"Why don't you invite him over so I can?"

"He's easily bored," I said.

"Then try to be interesting, Brenda Belle. Play one of your little piano pieces for him. Show him your avocado plants. I'll bake a chocolate ripple fudge cake for the occasion."

"I'll think about it," I said.

"Promise?"

"Yes," I said. "I'll think about it."

What I was really thinking about was what repulsive and revolting things Dr. Cutler was supposed to have done. He was a mild-mannered man, balding, bespectacled and bossed around by Christine's mother. A few years ago I owned a cat, and once when I took her to Dr. Cutler, I got a glimpse of that marriage. There was an intercom in his office which was connected with his house. Every few minutes Mrs. Cutler's voice would come blaring over the intercom. She was nagging at him about staying too late in his office; she was saying things like: "Ted, I'll give you three minutes to get here or we'll eat without you!" and "Ted, did you *hear* me?" There was an old ski cap of his hanging on a hook behind him, and finally he just put it over the intercom, as though he were pulling it down over her mouth. . . . I'd also heard that Ty Hardin's nickname for Mrs. Cutler was "Screamer."

For Christmas, my mother had ordered an electric blanket from Sears for my Aunt Faith. It was supposed to arrive by bus late that afternoon. Around five o'clock, my mother and I piled into her old Oldsmobile and headed for the depot.

"I always feel sorry for poor Faith at Christmas," my mother said en route. "I think of all the Christmases when you were a little tyke and poor Faith had no child."

"I know a lot of kids who plan never to get married," I said. Actually, I didn't, but I'd read about it in magazines.

"Every woman wants to get married, Brenda Belle."

"What about woman's liberation?"

"That's just television talk-show fantasy, Brenda Belle. That's just a lot of talk from New York City. Women are very hard there, and they're not typical. Actresses and slutty types."

"Maybe I'll move to New York after I get out of school," I said, thinking maybe I'd move to New York *before* I got out of school.

"You wouldn't be happy in a big city, dear. People aren't friendly, and all the men are married."

"Nobody'd nag me about getting married, though."

"Nobody will nag you here, either. Do you think I'm nagging you? Would you rather I just ignored you, and let you grow up to be some lonely woman who's missed out on life? Do you want to become someone like Ella Early?"

She didn't wait for my answer. She said, "If I didn't have you, Brenda Belle, I'd consider myself a failure."

"But what if I turn out bad?"

"I'm not going to let that happen," she said, giving my knee a little squeeze.

"There is such a thing as a dud avocado," I said. "You can lavish all the care in the world on it, but it just won't come up like the rest."

"You're not an avocado," my mother said, which was about the only reassuring word I'd heard all day.

After my mother parked the car, we walked down to the hotel on Central Avenue. The bus depot was next to the hotel. The bus was just pulling up when I saw Adam Blessing waiting near the benches out in front.

"That's Adam Blessing in the navy pea jacket," I said to my mother.

"This is your chance to introduce me," she said.

The bus was letting off passengers. I tried to get

Adam's attention by waving both my hands over my head.

My mother pulled down my left one. "Wave with one hand, not both," she said. "Don't appear too eager."

A woman in furs got off the bus, and Adam made a dive for her. They hugged each other and the woman kissed him several times on the cheek.

My mother said, "That woman looks very familiar."

She was a tall woman with golden hair, the sort of woman who looks like she's wallowing in money. The fur was mink. Her coat was open, and there was a huge gold necklace against a white cashmere sweater. She wore a black-and-white scarf with tiny red hearts on it, and her fingers were loaded with gold rings, one with an enormous diamond the size of a radish.

My mother and I stood right next to them.

"Oh, A.J.! A.J.! How good to see you!" the woman was shouting.

Then Adam looked up and saw me.

He looked flustered.

My mother was saying to herself, "I know her. I know I know her."

I knew I knew her, too.

"Hi, Adam!" I said.

"Hello, Brenda Belle."

"This is my mother," I said.

"How do you do, Mrs. Blossom," he said.

"I'm glad to meet you, Adam," she said. She looked at the woman then and said, "Aren't you—"

Adam interrupted. "This is Mrs. Waite. Mrs. Waite, this is Brenda Belle Blossom and Mrs. Blossom."

"How do you do," she said.

My mother said, "I could have sworn you were Billie Kay Case, the famous old-time movie actress."

Adam winced at the word "old-time."

Billie Kay Case smiled at my mother and said, "People are always telling me that. Thank you very much, but I'm afraid I have to disappoint you."

"It's a remarkable resemblance," my mother said. "Even your voice."

"Do you hear that, A.J.?" Billie Kay Case said to Adam. "I should be very flattered."

"I have a taxi waiting," Adam said. "Grandpa Blessing's expecting us, Mrs. Waite."

"Oh, no, honey, no!" Billie Kay Case said. "I'm not ready to meet your grandfather until tomorrow. I'm dead, honey. All I want is a hot bath in a quiet hotel room, and a whole evening with nothing to do."

"But he's made a punch and stuff to eat!" Adam protested.

"No way, honey," she said. "You just point me

toward the hotel and we'll call it a day for now. I need my beauty sleep."

"We trimmed a tree and everything," Adam kept protesting.

"You just get Janice down from the coat rack inside the bus, honey," she told Adam, "and that will be that for now. I can't meet the public when I've just popped off a Greyhound, love. You understand, love."

In an aside, my mother said, "Someone's probably told her too often that she resembles Billie Kay Case. She's beginning to believe it. She's picked up all her mannerisms. Pathetic."

I didn't say anything. I remembered that Adam had asked me not to tell anyone she was in Storm.

While Adam went inside the bus for whatever Janice was, I said, "Are you staying in Storm long, Mrs. Waite?"

"No. Only through tomorrow," she said.

My mother said, "I guess I'd better ask the driver about our package," and she went around to the back of the bus.

Billie Kay Case asked me, "Are you a friend of Adam's, dear?"

"I guess I'm his best friend in Storm," I said, wanting her to like me. I was really excited, knowing who she was and having it a secret.

"Then you should take my place tonight," Billie

Kay Case said. She looked over her shoulder at Adam, who was coming out of the bus carrying a small animal case. "Adam!" she called out. "I have a divine idea!"

"What is it?" he said, setting the case down on the snowy sidewalk.

"Not on the sidewalk, honey," Billie Kay Case said. "I don't want Janice to freeze. Pick her up, love. . . . Listen, sweetheart, why don't you invite Betty Belle here to take my place tonight?"

"*Brenda* Belle," I said.

"She's going to a party," he said.

"No, I'm not," I said. "I was uninvited."

"You were invited," he said. "You told me so."

"Then I was uninvited," I said.

"You see, love?" Billie Kay Case said. "It works out perfectly! Betty Belle will go back in the taxi with you."

"She can't," Adam said. "She's with her mother."

My mother suddenly materialized. "I couldn't help overhearing," she said (she never could), "and I think that's a lovely idea. You have my permission, dear."

"Perfect!" Billie Kay Case said. "Then it's all settled."

"I don't think he wants—" I tried to say.

"Fine!" my mother interrupted. "Don't stay too late, dear."

68

From the Journal of A.

I was disappointed that Billie Kay wouldn't come back with me, because I had an idea Grandpa Blessing was really looking forward to meeting her.

"Does she go under the name 'Mrs. Waite' a lot?" Brenda Belle asked me in the taxi.

"Well, she used to be married to this man who was never around," I said. "She was always waiting for him, and we got the idea to call her 'Mrs. Waite' then."

"I know who she married," Brenda Belle said. Then she named my father.

"Yeah," I said. "That's who she married. I was their neighbor."

"Did you ever meet him, Adam?"

"Sure," I said. "I told you. We were neighbors."

"Oh wow! What's *he* like?"

"He's like anyone," I said.

"He's *not* like anyone," Brenda Belle said. "How could he be like anyone? He's practically more important than the President of the United States of America!"

"Okay," I said. "He is a big man. I won't deny that. His jokes are always funny, even when they're not."

"What does that remark mean?" Brenda Belle asked me.

"It's something he used to say about rich people," I told her. "It's a verse he liked to recite. 'Money is honey, my little sonny, and a rich man's joke is always funny.'"

Brenda Belle sighed. She said, "You've had kind of an interesting life, haven't you, Adam? I mean, being expelled from a private school, and living next door to famous people. Nothing much has happened in my life. That's why I'm such a mess."

"You're not a mess," I said. "Anyway, maybe things will start to happen."

"That's unlikely," she said. "Do you feel like you've been forced into this evening by my mother and Billie Kay?"

"No, I don't feel that way," I said. "It is Christmas Eve, after all. And my grandfather *is* expecting company."

"I'm glad that I refused to go to Christine Cutler's," she said.

"You said you were uninvited."

"I just said that because my mother and Billie Kay were standing there," she said. "The truth is I refused to go. I said that I wouldn't go anywhere where you weren't wanted."

"Really?" I looked at her with an uncontrollable smile tipping my lips.

"Certainly," she said. "One thing I am is loyal."

I reached over and took her hand. I'm a real sucker for loyalty. I'm a loyalty freak. I've seen too many examples of people not sticking up for their own, or people walking out on their own, or people just forgetting their own. I believe you ought to stand by, stick with and stay near the people you picked out to be your friends or your lovers. With relatives, it's different, maybe; you can't always put your heart in it because you never chose them, but you shouldn't let anyone trash your own blood either, unless you're related to men who run wars or women who're mean to little children, people like that.

"Brenda Belle," I said, "stay around."

"I'm not going anywhere," she said.

When we arrived at my grandfather's, he wasn't there. There was this note on the kitchen table:

I am off paying my Christmas respects to old friends. Please enjoy my home, punch bowl and repast. Season's Greetings. C.B.

71

The words didn't even sound like Grandpa Blessing; they sounded stilted and phony, and I realized he probably imagined I'd read the note to Billie Kay. I wondered who he meant by "old friends," since as far as I knew, my grandfather had no friends in Storm.

"What repast is he referring to?" Brenda Belle asked me. "I'm starving."

"It's just some salami and some cheese and hard bread," I said.

"I'd love to," Brenda Belle said.

"I guess Grandpa decided to give me time to be with Billie Kay alone."

"I'll bet this is the dullest Christmas she's ever spent," said Brenda Belle. "No offense, Adam, but you know what I mean."

Then she saw the tree. "Oh my Glory! Adam! Beer cans!"

"We made it," I said defensively. "We like it."

Brenda Belle began this little conversation with herself and her imitation of her mother. "Did you have a good time, dear? . . . Oh my yes, Mother, we sat before the tree of beer cans! . . . I beg your pardon, dear, I thought you said something that sounded like— . . . Beer cans, Mother? . . . Yes, I thought you said beer cans."

I said, "I suppose your tree has the usual five-and-ten crap hanging off it, hmmm?"

"Of course not," she said, "we decided to trim ours, this year, with old banana peels." She threw her parka across for me to catch and hang in the closet.

"Banana peels are such old hat," I said, "I heard the Cutlers did their tree in carrot tops."

"Not true," she trilled back at me, "simply not true. I have it on the best authority that the Cutler tree is trimmed with turtle turds."

"Ah, turtle turds," I said. "Tinseled, too, I trust."

"Indubitably!" said Brenda Belle. "Did your grandfather mention a punch bowl as well as a repast?"

"Indeed he did," I said.

"Fantastico!" she said. "Joy-ex Noel, Adam Blessing."

"Hark the Herald," I said.

It was a very strong punch, but I was fighting back because I was a little concerned about my grandfather. I wanted to be sober if he came home with a load on.

Brenda Belle was tossing them back at a fairly fast clip.

"Adam," she asked me, "I want your honest opinion on something."

"All right. On what?"

"On me. Did it ever cross your mind for one minute, one half a teeny tiny second even, that there might be a certain mix-up in my genes?"

"I've never even seen you in your jeans," I said.

"G-e-n-e-s, Adam. Not blue jeans. Human genes."

"What do you mean a mix-up?"

"A confusion," she said, "as though my body wasn't sure what I was supposed to be."

"I don't get you."

"Do you think of me as a feminine being?"

"Yes."

"Totally?"

"Yes," I said, "totally."

"You don't think there are masculine under-tones?"

I had to laugh at that idea.

She shoved her elbow into my chest. "Don't laugh! I'm serious!"

"I'm not laughing at *you*. I'm laughing at that idea. Whose idea is that?"

"My mother suspects I'm slightly unnatural," she said.

"Did she *say* that?"

Then she just started bawling. "No, she didn't say that, she didn't have to say that. I'm a social flop. It's obvious. I don't have dates, telephone calls. I don't get valentines. I'm a zero."

"Isn't it a little early to decide that, Brenda Belle?"

"A little too Ella Early?" she said. "Not where mater is concerned. Old mater is afeared I am a trick of nature."

"Don't cry," I said.

"That's why I have this scabby mustache. I was trying to correct nature's nasty."

"Brenda Belle," I said, "I'm nothing too."

"At least you know what sex you are."

"I know what sex you are, too," I said. "Brenda Belle, please don't cry. I have an idea. We could make a pact."

"What kind of a pact?" she whined.

"We could stick by each other. We could stick by each other and be friends to all the nothings. We could establish Nothing Power."

"We could go steady."

"What?"

"I said, could we go steady?"

"Why not?" I shrugged. "We could say we were going steady."

"We *could*?"

"Sure," I said.

"Then we're really going steady?"

"Sure."

"Nothing Power!" Brenda Belle said. "What a neat idea!"

"We'll start a campaign," I said. "We'll give Nothing Power to everyone who's miserable."

"We'll write a mash note to Ella Early from anonymous," she said.

"We'll tell that crabby bus driver he's great!" I said.

"You mean Rufus Kerin?" she said.

"Sure. Is that his name, the one who always shouts, 'Have your money ready, dumbbells!'?"

"That's Rufus! Oh my Glory, no one's ever had a kind word for Rufus Kerin!"

"We'll shower him with affection," I said. "We'll fawn over him!"

"And Marilyn Pepper, because she has acne so bad!"

"Absolutely!" I said.

"We're going steady," she said. "This is the happiest Christmas of my entire life!"

"You have Nothing Power!" I said.

"You have to give me something," she said. "A ring or something. What do you have?"

The telephone rang.

"Just a minute," I said as I went out to the kitchen to answer the phone. I lifted the receiver and a man's voice said, "Is your grandfather Charlie Blessing?"

"Yes," I said. "Is he all right?"

"He's got a load on, but he's all right. We threw him in a cab. He's broke. He owes a bar bill of a little over eight bucks."

"Who is this?" I said.

"This is Sampson's Bar on Swift Avenue. The old man's been sopping it up for hours. We threw him in a cab."

"I hope you didn't *throw* him in a cab," I said. "I

hope you walked him gently to a cab, since he was your customer!"

"Some customer!" the man said. "He owes a bar bill here!"

"So what?" I said. "You sold him the booze on credit, didn't you?"

"Look, buddy, we didn't have to take care of Charlie. We could have left him to freeze in a snow-drift, wouldn't be the first time he's slept outdoors, but it's Christmas Eve, so we thought we'd help the old—"

"Thanks and go to hell!" I hollered. I was still shaking after I slammed down the receiver.

Behind me, Brenda Belle said, "Who did you say that to?"

"A good samaritan," I said snidely. "My grandfather's coming home in a taxi. I have to get some money ready."

"Is he drunk again?"

"Why the hell do you have to say that?" I said. "He could have been run over, or had a heart attack —any number of reasons!"

"It's just that he's often drunk," Brenda Belle said.

"You're like everyone else in this stinking town!" I said. "The damn bartender gives him drinks on credit, lets him get soused, then looks down on him because he gets drunk! And *you* say right off the bat that he's loaded!"

"I didn't say it," she said. "I asked it. . . . What do *I* care if Charlie's drunk again? I'm not completely sober myself."

"DON'T CALL MY GRANDFATHER BY HIS FIRST NAME!" I shouted. "And don't say drunk *again*." I slumped down in the kitchen chair. "Look," I said, "if we're going to establish Nothing Power around here, it begins at home, like charity. . . . My poor grandfather."

"I'm sorry," she said. "I am. I hope Dr. Blessing is all right."

"I'm just glad Billie Kay isn't here," I said.

"I'm really sorry," Brenda Belle said. "Are we still going steady?"

"Yes," I said, "but try to think before you shoot off your big mouth again."

"I intend to," said Brenda Belle.

When a horn honked in the yard, I reached for my coat. The two-fifty I had left over from my weekly allowance was in the pocket. I'd been planning to buy something for my grandfather with it, a bottle of good wine or some expensive pipe tobacco. I grabbed the money and went out to pay for the taxi. So much for his Christmas remembrance, I told myself. He'd been insisting he didn't want anything anyway.

My grandfather was all dressed up. He had on a double-breasted pin-striped suit that had seen better days, a blue shirt with a round white collar, a polka-dot tie and a black wool scarf. His coat didn't match his outfit: he was wearing a short plaid lumber jacket.

"You didn't have to come out and meet me, A.J.," he said, ignoring the fact that the driver was waiting to be paid. "Go back to your guest. I'll be no trouble." He was talking in that strange, stilted way he'd written the note.

I shoved the money at the cab driver. "Enough?" I asked.

"Yes," he said. Then he turned and said, "Charlie, want me to help you in?"

"Help me?" my grandfather said, as though he'd received a slap in the face. "I'm not in my grave yet."

"I didn't mean that, Charlie," the driver said. "I meant you had a little too much Christmas cheer."

"Nonsense," said my grandfather. He stepped out of the cab and made his way stiffly across the yard, weaving slightly.

I waved the taxi driver on and went alongside my grandfather to take his arm. He shook my hand away. "Do you think I'm an incompetent, too?"

"No, sir. I was just helping you."

"Well, I happen to hate help!"

"Yes, sir. I won't help you then."

"I don't hate helping but I hate help. Is that clear?"

"Perfectly," I said.

I opened the door and he walked into the kitchen, standing before Brenda Belle, swaying a bit like some tall Georgia pine shaking in the breeze.

"Why, Faith!" he said.

"Welcome to Time Tunnel," I said to Brenda Belle. "Welcome to the Distant Past."

"Hello, Dr. Blessing," Brenda Belle said.

"You and Hank know how to laugh," my grandfather said, "and that's more important than anything else. Millie never makes him laugh. She doesn't have that gift."

Then my grandfather walked into the living room, stretched out on the couch in his coat, and passed out.

I walked Brenda Belle up the hill to her house.

"I'm sorry Christmas Eve had to be cut short," I said.

"He called it a gift," Brenda Belle said. "Making someone laugh is a gift. I never thought of that."

"He liked your father a lot," I said.

"I'll bet he didn't like my mother."

"He doesn't dislike your mother. . . . He just said your father and your aunt laughed a lot together."

"Boy, I bet that really made my mother mad," Brenda Belle said.

"I don't know," I said.

Then she said, "Be thinking about what you're going to give me to prove we're going steady. Ty Hardin gave Christine Cutler his football letter, and a little gold football she wears on a chain."

"I'll be thinking," I said.

"I'm going to work on a mash note for Ella Early, too." Brenda Belle giggled and squeezed my arm. "Nothing Power is the greatest invention since sliced bread!" she said.

"It'll have to be our Christmas gift to each other," I told her, "because I'm flat broke."

"Merry Christmas," Brenda Belle said. We were in front of her door. "Merry Christmas and a real Nothing New Year!"

Notes for a Novel by B.B.B.

"I don't see how you can be going steady so suddenly," my mother said. "Nothing happened last night, did it, Brenda Belle?"

I realized a strange thing when she said that: Adam and I hadn't even kissed.

"Nothing like *that*," I said. "We just kissed."

"Are you sure?"

"Of course I'm sure."

"You were very talkative when you came in," my mother said.

"What has that got to do with anything?"

"Well, you mentioned that you had a little punch. Are you sure you *remember* everything that happened?"

"Mother," I said, "we didn't have sex. I'd have remembered that."

"Don't say that, Brenda Belle!"

"What? Don't say what?"

"S-e-x," my mother said.

"We didn't have relations," I said. "We didn't make o-u-t."

"No one buys the cow if he can get the milk free," my mother said.

"Thanks a lot," I said. "Mooooooo."

"I'm sorry, dear. It's just that I'm a little bewildered. He didn't even give you a Christmas gift, did he?"

"He will," I lied. I planned to buy myself a box of candy in Corps and say Adam gave it to me.

"And what about your gift for him?" she said.

"I'm going to give him a plant," I said.

That was sort of true, even though it wasn't a plant yet. It was still a sweet potato. I decided to take it right down to him without being asked, because I was afraid that if I called, he'd say not to come. I didn't completely trust Nothing Power yet, and I wanted to see Billie Kay Case again.

I arrived about two thirty that Christmas afternoon.

Dr. Blessing answered the door. "Come in," he said. "Are you a friend of Adam's?"

He didn't even remember our meeting the night before.

"I'm Adam's girlfriend," I said. "Brenda Belle Blossom."

"Of course," he said. "You look a lot like your Aunt Faith. . . . Adam's on the phone, talking to his father," he said as we walked through the kitchen. I could see Adam standing over near the refrigerator, hunched over the telephone receiver.

"Come in and meet Mrs. Waite," Dr. Blessing said.

"That's all right," I said. "I know who she really is. Adam told me all about being her neighbor."

Billie Kay Case smiled up at me as I entered the living room.

"Well, hi, Betty Belle," she said.

"Brenda Belle," I said. "Is that Janice?"

"Yes, dis is my little snookums, Danice," she said. She was holding this Siamese cat that was trying hard to get away. There were scratches on her arm. "Little Danice is a-fwaid of trangers," she said. The cat spat at her. She slapped its nose.

Dr. Blessing was walking around the room wearing the same suit and tie he'd had on the night before. He kept clearing his throat nervously and frowning across at Billie Kay and her cat.

There was a certain amount of tension in the room, but I couldn't figure out what was causing it.

I said, "You two go right on talking. Don't mind me."

"We weren't talking," Billie Kay said. "Dr. Blessing doesn't have a lot to say to me."

"That's not quite true," Dr. Blessing said.

From the kitchen I could hear Adam say, "I don't care if your package is late. Stop apologizing, Dad."

Billie Kay Case told Dr. Blessing, "Well, if it's not quite true that you don't have anything to say to me, by all means say what you have to say. You seem to be building up to something."

"I'm not building up to anything," Dr. Blessing said.

"I'm getting bad vibes," Billie Kay said. "I've only been here half an hour and I'm getting bad vibes already." She was still trying to handle the Siamese, holding it down like her hand was a weight.

"I've seen a few of your old movies," I said. "My Aunt Faith is a real fan of yours."

"You look a lot like your Aunt Faith," Dr. Blessing told me again.

The cat jumped out of Billie Kay's grasp, ran toward the curtains and climbed them. Billie Kay ran after her.

Then Dr. Blessing snapped. "Leave her *alone!*"

"Wh-what?" Billie Kay turned around and stared at him, as though she'd never been spoken to that way in all her life.

"I said leave her *alone!*"

"I heard what you said but I don't believe my own ears," Billie Kay said. She was wearing this red velvet pants suit and her face was turning a matching shade of red.

From the kitchen, Adam was saying, "Dad, I

didn't expect you to come here. I *know* you're busy!"

Dr. Blessing was facing Billie Kay, his own face red, too. His hands were balled to fists at his side, and his voice shook as he spoke. "All right!" he said. "I'll say what I have to say! A cat owner who has scratches on her arms shouldn't own a cat! A cat doesn't scratch unless it's being hurt or terrified! A cat—"

Billie Kay didn't let him finish. "Now you listen to me, Mr. Know-It-All! These little scratches are from the game that Janice and I play! I tickle her stomach and she scratches."

"That's *your* little game," Dr. Blessing said. "It isn't the cat's idea of a game, or she wouldn't scratch you. You tickle her too hard! How would you like some monster fifty times your size digging her fingers into *your* belly? That's what it feels like to that poor creature! You don't know how to handle a cat; you shouldn't own a cat!"

"Why, you old drunk," Billie Kay said. "Who are you to tell *anyone* how to handle *anything?*"

"I am a doctor of veterinary medicine!" he said. "And I happen to be sober enough to see why that cat is a nervous wreck! Leave her the hell alone! Stop using her like a goddamn toy! Let the creature relax! Let her sleep without you mauling her! Let her sit for a while and clean herself without you picking her up and messing up her fur! If you want something you can hug and lavish attention on, get a big hound dog! That's a little creature up there on the curtains!"

Billie Kay sat down on the couch shaking her head from side to side. "You are something," she said. "You are something to write home about, Mr. Doctor Blessing! That cat is my treasure. I would no more hurt that cat than I would put my own hand in fire!"

"She's not a relaxed animal, anyone can see that," Dr. Blessing said. "She won't even come to you when you call her."

"Cats don't!" Billie Kay said.

"Cats *do*, if you treat them properly. That little thing is practically wild."

"She's high-strung," said Billie Kay. "She's Siamese."

"You're high-strung," Dr. Blessing said, "and she reflects it!"

I said, "It must be wonderful to be an old movie star." I was hoping to break up the argument.

"You can see how wonderful it is," Billie Kay said. "You can see how much respect an *old* movie star gets."

"You're younger than I am," Dr. Blessing said.

"God himself is younger than you are," Billie Kay said. "Methuselah is younger than you are."

Adam walked into the room at that point. "What's all the shouting about?" he said.

"She asked for conversation and she got it," Dr. Blessing said.

"It's such gracious conversation, too," Billie Kay said.

"What's Janice doing up on the curtains?" Adam asked.

"Trying to escape before she's tickled to death," Dr. Blessing said.

"Are you two fighting?" Adam asked.

"Oh, no, love," Billie Kay answered. "We're just having a friendly discussion about the fact I'm not a fit person to own a cat!"

"Grandpa!" Adam said. "Why would you say something like that?"

"Because I don't like cruelty to animals!" he said.

"Never mind *people*!" Billie Kay said.

"People can take care of themselves," Dr. Blessing snapped.

I said, "I brought you a Christmas present, Adam, to celebrate our going steady."

"Adam!" Billie Kay exclaimed. "What nice news!"

"Congratulations," Dr. Blessing mumbled as he passed us on his way into the kitchen. "That calls for a beer."

"Doesn't everything?" Billie Kay said sarcastically.

He began slamming things around in the kitchen, and Billie Kay leaned forward and beckoned Adam and me closer. "Why don't you two go for a walk?"

she said. "You probably want to spend a little time alone together on Christmas Day. Dinner won't be ready for hours."

"No, really," Adam said. "We can see each other all the time. We'll stay right here."

"A.J.," Billie Kay said, "take Betty Belle for a walk!"

"Honestly, Billie Kay," Adam said, "we *want* to stay here."

"I don't want you to!" she said. "I have a few things to get off my chest with that ornery character in the kitchen!"

"He doesn't mean what he's saying," Adam said.

"Oh, yes, he does! And I mean what I'm going to say to him!"

"She wants us to go, Adam," I said.

"Just blow, A.J.! Come back in about an hour!"

We walked along Ski Tow Avenue in the bright sun.

"I hope they'll be all right together," Adam said.

"My present for you is this sweet potato," I said, taking it out of my coat pocket and handing it to him.

"Fine, fine," he laughed. "I have some old coffee grounds for you."

"You don't understand," I said. "I'm not kidding. You put this in a glass of water, stick in three toothpicks so it'll hang in the glass, and it'll begin to sprout

89

green buds in no time. It has Nothing Power."

"Thanks," he said. "I'll try it." He put the potato in his coat.

"It'll be a gorgeous plant before you know it," I said, "and you can pot it. I have a reason for giving it to you, aside from Nothing Power."

"What is it?"

"Since we're going steady now, I'm teaching you about beautiful things . . . since I'm not a beautiful thing."

"I don't get you, Brenda Belle."

"This will become a beautiful thing, but after it's a beautiful thing for a while, it'll change," I said.

"How will it change?"

"It'll begin to stink," I said. "It will make you realize that beauty is not that big a deal, just in case you wish you were going steady with a beauty contest winner."

Adam laughed. "I'm satisfied with you, Brenda Belle."

"That's another thing. Try to call me 'honey' or 'darling' or something besides my name. It won't be believable if you don't."

"I'll try," he said.

"And I'll need something of yours. How about that ring you're wearing?"

"It's my father's ring," he said.

"Adam, it's just a loan."

"Okay," he said. "I guess it'll be okay." He took it off and handed it to me. "Don't lose it, though. It was his school ring."

"You can have it back anytime you ask for it," I said. I tried it on, but it was too big. I planned to put it on a chain and wear it around my neck.

I said, "What does your father do, Adam?"

"He travels around a lot."

"Is he a traveling salesman?"

"You could say that."

"My father was in the rodeo," I said. "He was a star."

"That's very exciting," Adam said.

"I'm not saying my father was better than your father because mine was a star and yours is just a salesman, but sometimes blood will tell."

"I suppose so," Adam said.

"My secret desire is probably to be a writer," I said. "I keep these notebooks I call 'Notes for a Novel' and I write down everything that happens—when anything happens, which it doesn't often."

I caught a glimpse of Ty Hardin walking toward us. He was probably coming from Christine Cutler's.

Adam was saying, "I don't know what I'll be. I used to want to be a doctor. An M.D. . . . . But I hate science."

Ty Hardin is just about THE most handsome boy in Storm, and maybe in all of Burlington County.

He's a towhead, and his hair is silky and longer than other boys' hair. Everything about Ty is a little more special than the others, including, I suppose, his girlfriend, initials: C.C.

"Here comes Ty Hardin," said Adam.

"Big deal," I said, but I was by no means immune to Tyrone Hardin. As he came closer, I felt suddenly tongue-tied, rubber-kneed, gross.

"Merry Christmas, Ty!" said Adam.

"Hi, Adam, Brenda Belle. Merry Christmas."

My mouth got loose from my mind. "Well, how was the old Noel party at the Cutlers'?" I asked him.

Ty made a face. He said, "Snore."

I laughed and laughed.

Ty put his folded hands up under his chin and made ZZZZZ noises.

I cracked up again.

Adam said, "It was boring, huh?"

I said, "Oh no, it was fab, wasn't it, Ty? It was marvy. It was a barrel of, huh, Ty?" I nudged his ribs with my elbow.

"It was a barrel of, all right," he smiled at me.

I laughed again, holding my sides because they were beginning to hurt. "Another gala evening at Christine Cutler's, wheeeeee!"

"Well, see you," Ty said, passing us with a little wave.

"Not if we see you first!" I called back. Then I

shouted after him, "Hey, Ty! We're an item! Adam and I are going steady!"

He turned around and bowed. "Wheeeeeeee! Another gala romance," he said in a flat tone. Then he went on down the road.

"I think they had a fight!" I said. "My Glory be!"

"What do you care?" Adam said.

"I don't," I said.

"She probably didn't want me to come to her party because my grandfather and her father don't get along," he said.

I felt guilty that I'd ever told him that, but not guilty enough to admit the truth. I said, "Anyway, my mother knows things about Dr. Cutler that are repulsive and revolting."

"What things?" said Adam.

"I don't know, she won't say. . . . Hey, Adam," I said. "He deserves Nothing Power, too. Dr. Cutler. I mean, if he's done repulsive and revolting things, he deserves it, too. Plus the fact his wife is a terrible nag."

"We'll make a list right after the holidays," said Adam. "Meanwhile, have you written Ella Early that mash note?"

"Me?" I said, "Me? Why do I have to write another female a mash note? With my inferiority complex on that subject, that isn't fair, even or equal!"

"Life isn't fair, even or equal. I told you that,"

Adam said. "You said you'd write it, so write it. You're the one who wants to be a writer."

"Dear Ella Early," I said. "This is your secret admirer, the dry cleaner. I have fallen in love with the smell of chalk dust on your dresses."

From the Journal of A.

We didn't wait for the holidays to end to establish Nothing Power. We decided that during the holidays was a perfect time to launch our campaign, since miserable people were all the more miserable between Christmas and New Year's.

Our campaign began modestly with four undertakings.

1. Ella Early: Brenda Belle composed a brilliant mash note from an anonymous student. She made it sound as though he truly idolized her, and that because of her he wanted to become a world-famous scientist. He explained that he was much too shy to identify himself, but that he hung on her every word in class: She was his inspiration in life. We mailed it to the rooming house where Ella Early lived.

2. Marilyn Pepper: I picked out a Hallmark card, one of those "From Your Secret Friend" kind. It had a very sentimental verse, all about "and I think of you each night until the morning light." We put a question mark where a name would ordinarily go, and sent it to her home.

3. Dr. Cutler: Brenda Belle found an old-fashioned postcard printed in the year 1927. She bought it at Modell's Antique Nook for seventy-five cents. There were three big red roses across the front, and the words: WHEREVER THIS MAY FIND YOU, I TRUST IT WILL REMIND YOU, OF ONE YOU LEFT BEHIND YOU. Brenda Belle figured that ought to make Mrs. Cutler appreciate him. . . . We didn't sign it; we just sent it to him at home.

4. Rufus Kerin: We simply asked him to the New Year's Eve party.

The New Year's Eve party was Billie Kay's idea. At that point, everything going on at my grandfather's was her idea, from the idea she was going to stay in Storm for a while longer to the idea my grandfather was going to give up drinking while she was there.

Billie Kay had taken over. She had driven down to Burlington one afternoon to shop for "a few new outfits" to wear while she stayed in Storm. She also came back with a sport coat for my grandfather, some new slacks and shirts for him, and a bright red V-neck cashmere sweater for me.

"I don't see how you're going to keep your identity a secret at this party," I told her on the morning of New Year's Eve. "Everyone is going to recognize you."

"You let me worry about that," she said. "I can always handle that situation."

We were making sandwiches in the kitchen the afternoon of the party, and she was waiting for the taxi to take her back to the hotel for some beauty sleep before the big event.

My grandfather was making a pot of Boston baked beans. He'd made them for me the first night I'd arrived in Storm. I remember that he'd called Late Night Larry that night, to explain the difference between New England cooking and Southern cooking. ("The old New England households had one hired girl, at best, to do all the chores. A lot of New England dishes are the kind you don't have to watch. They just boil on top of the stove. But the old Southern households had a lot of Negro slaves, and that's why Southern cooking is more complicated, with fried foods and recipes that require watching." . . . "Why, thank you, Chuck From Vermont. What a fascinating morsel, ha ha, to pass on to Radioland!")

I'd been trying to get my grandfather to talk that way around Billie Kay, so she could see how interesting he was. I'd throw him some cues, but he wouldn't pick up on them. For days, he'd been clammed up.

"Tell Billie Kay about the fine for celebrating Christmas," I tried again while we were waiting for her taxi.

My grandfather just shrugged.

"Has the liquor bottle got your tongue?" Billie Kay asked him.

"No one's got yours," he said.

Billie Kay had bet him he couldn't go a whole week without something to drink. He'd bet her she couldn't go a whole week without picking up Janice. Janice was living with us temporarily. When Billie Kay was around, Janice hid under my grandfather's bed. Nights she came out and sat on his lap.

Our party was to be sort of an open-house type. Young and old were invited. Billie Kay had called Mrs. Blossom to spread the word, and Brenda Belle herself had been calling kids from school.

"No tasting the punch, either," Billie Kay told my grandfather. "I'll oversee the punch myself."

When the telephone rang, Billie Kay said, "A.J., I bet that's your father. He'll probably want to say hello to me, too, since he didn't get the chance Christmas day."

My grandfather went to answer the phone. I didn't tell Billie Kay that when my father had called Christmas day, he'd said he had nothing to say to her. ("What the hell is she bothering you for?" he'd said. I'd said, "She's visiting. It's Christmas." He'd said, "Can't she find anyplace else to go?")

My father was in Los Angeles by then. We'd read in the newspapers that he was dating some new starlet the gossip columnists had nicknamed "Electric Socket," because her real name was Electra. I'd seen a picture of her. She was like a lot of girls my father was interested in: barely out of her teens, blonde, gigantic bust. It was hard to imagine him taking her to meet all the important people he knew—governors and senators and past presidential candidates, plus the whole Hollywood crowd my father hung around with. Billie Kay said Electric Socket was just "dressing." Billie Kay said that at the gatherings my father attended, the less a woman knew, the better.

It was not my father calling.

"If he's not eating," my grandfather was telling someone, "don't try and force him to eat. Have you taken his temperature?"

Billie Kay marched herself into the kitchen and took the phone right out of his hands. "We do not give free advice on animal care here," she said into it. "If your animal is ill, take your animal to Dr. Cutler and pay the fee." Then she put down the receiver.

"What'd you do that for?" my grandfather snarled at her.

"For your self-respect," said Billie Kay. "I'm tired of these freeloaders who call up here every time one of their pets gets the sniffles or the runs!"

My grandfather shook his head from side to side.

"I'd forgotten what it was like having a woman around," he said. "I'd forgotten what meddlers they all are."

"You've also forgotten how to talk to a woman," Billie Kay said. "You've hardly said two words to me since I got here this morning."

"The two words I'd choose to say would be 'go away,'" said my grandfather.

"I'm going away in about five minutes, but I'm coming back!"

"We won't be on pins and needles waiting," he said.

After she left in the taxi, my grandfather sat in the living room for a while, pretending to watch an old movie on television. I felt sorry for him. He was fidgeting and sighing and rubbing his chin with his fingers.

"If you want to sneak a beer," I said, "I won't tell her."

"A bargain's a bargain," he said. "A bet's a bet."

"I'm sorry she's so bossy," I said. "She wasn't bossy toward my father."

"She wasn't herself with your father. She was trying to be a girl again."

"Don't let it get you down," I said. "She'll be gone in a few days."

"That sport ccat she bought me," said my grandfather. "I once owned just such a coat. It's too good for me now."

"Why is it too good for you?"

"I mean I don't have any place to wear it!" he grumbled.

"You can wear a coat like that anywhere," I said.

"Around here they'll think I'm putting on the dog."

"What do you care what they think around here?"

"I happen to live here, A.J.!" he shouted.

There wasn't anything I could say to that. It was strange. He didn't seem to care that the local bartender threw him into a cab after a drinking bout, but he cared if people thought he was putting on the dog.

"I'm sorry, A.J.," he said. "It's just that I am what I am, as Popeye the Sailor would say. I yam what I yam and that's all what I yam."

"I get you," I said.

"I'm too old to change," he said.

"You don't have to change, Grandpa."

"What do *you* know?" he said softly. "What do you know about it, A.J.?"

He didn't expect an answer, and I didn't have one.

We worked all afternoon cleaning up the place. We washed out a dozen old jelly jars for extra glasses.

101

(I had to hand it to Billie Kay. She wasn't the snob I'd thought she might be about my grandfather's hospitality. She didn't act at all uncomfortable eating off plates that didn't match, or drinking coffee from cracked mugs, and she'd actually raved over our tree.) By the time Brenda Belle telephoned around five o'clock, the place was really shipshape. If it wasn't fancy, it was clean and orderly.

"I've got great news," she said. "Ty Hardin is coming, darling."

I still had trouble getting used to her calling me "darling" and "sweetheart." It was hard for me to use words like that, too.

"Fine, honey bunch," I said to her, trying not to sound too interested in the news Ty Hardin was coming. I'd been hoping Christine would come.

Brenda Belle immediately put a pin in that balloon. "He's not bringing Christine. They've had another big fight, and he's just ditching her on New Year's Eve. . . . Don't call me 'honey bunch,' darling. It's icky."

"Didn't you invite her anyway?" I said.

"Of course not! She's really a rotten person inside."

"I thought you liked her at one time."

"Christine Cutler?" she said. "You've got to be kidding, sweetheart. She's really this big phony, darling. I hate a phony!"

While she rattled off the names of the other people

102

coming, I thought of Christine being without a date on New Year's Eve. I felt badly for her, even though she had tried to keep me from attending her Christmas Eve party.

"Listen, love," I managed. "What about Nothing Power? A girl who's ditched on New Year's Eve certainly qualifies for Nothing Power."

"People who are Something to begin with don't deserve Nothing Power," said Brenda Belle. "Ty is a real character, sweetheart. When I called him he asked me if anyone ever mistook me for a boy over the telephone. You want to know what I said back?"

"What?"

"I said, 'No, has anyone ever mistaken you for one?' We both just howled then."

"I thought you were sensitive on that subject," I said.

"Not with Ty," she said, "because I know he really likes girls. I mean, he's had a lot of experience. He's the passionate type."

"I see," I said, but I didn't.

"Not that I care, but you're not exactly that type," Brenda Belle said. "You're younger . . . not just in years, but in a lot of ways."

I didn't argue with that. I'd driven down to Tijuana with my father that past summer, over a weekend. He'd insisted it was time for me to become a man. I'd become one, I suppose, at least in his eyes. Afterward, I'd paid this young girl with the money

103

he'd given me, and for some reason I'd said to her, "I'm sorry." My father heard about it from the woman who ran the place. She'd laughed when she told him, but my father didn't think it was funny. On the way back he'd bawled me out. "You have no game in you, A.J.! You have no adventure! That little bimbo was taking you for twenty bucks, and *you* apologized to *her*! Grow up, A.J.! Don't be so naïve!"

Brenda Belle said, "Before you hang up, sweetheart, there's one other thing. We're supposed to go into a clinch at the dot of midnight. People will expect that. I mean, we are going steady, darling."

"Okay," I said.

"Promise me you'll remember that, or I'll be humiliated," she said.

"I'll remember," I said. "I would have done it anyway."

"I can't disappoint my fans," she said. "And speaking of fans, lover, is it still a secret about Billie Kay?"

"Yes," I said.

"Then don't turn on the late show," she said. "One of her old movies with Bing Crosby is scheduled."

"Who'd turn on television in the middle of a party?" I answered.

Who'd turn on television in the middle of a party? Billie Kay Case would. Billie Kay Case did, promptly at eleven thirty.

It was then that I realized something I should have guessed from past experience with celebrities. They can stand being anonymous for just so long. They can go through the sunglasses bit and the false name bit for just so long, and then they get an itch for a little more attention than an ordinary person gets.

My father is the same way. One of his tricks used to be to get me to telephone a tip to the press that he was dining at a certain restaurant. Then when the photographers would show up, he'd make this big scene. He'd blame the maitre d', and he'd pretend he was escaping through a back door, and for good measure sometimes he'd break one of the photographers' cameras.

Billie Kay had her own sly approach that night. "Hey," she said, "don't we want to see the big Times Square scene, and the old red ball that drops at midnight?"

Then she turned on the set and switched to the channel where her old movie was showing.

"That's a Billie Kay Case movie coming on!" Brenda Belle's aunt cried out.

"Surprise! Surprise!" said Billie Kay. She had been dipping into the punch bowl, and she was feeling no pain.

"I think you really *are* Billie Kay Case," said Brenda Belle's mother.

"Surprise, surprise," Billie Kay answered, performing a small curtsy.

"I just knew it!" Brenda Belle's aunt squealed. She grabbed Billie Kay and hugged her, and then she called out, "Folks, we have a celebrity in our midst!"

I was standing by the Christmas tree with Brenda Belle and Ty Hardin. Brenda Belle had been paying more attention to Ty Hardin than to anyone, all the while calling me "darling" and "sweetheart" in these asides, but never taking her eyes from Ty.

Up until this point, Ty had been making fun of the tree and the jelly glasses we were serving the punch in. He was whispering his wisecracks to Brenda Belle, and she was giggling encouragement. I was really angry with her for not sticking up for my grandfather and me, and for not at least admitting that the tree was original, as she had when she first saw it. She was certainly spitting in the eye of Nothing Power.

When Ty heard the announcement that Billie Kay Case was present, he turned to me and said, "She's joking, right?"

Brenda Belle said, "It happens to be true, Ty. Billie Kay's a friend of ours, isn't she, darling?"

I gave her a dirty look. The tree and the jelly glasses weren't "ours," but Billie Kay Case *was* "ours."

"Why the sour look, sweetheart?" she asked.

Ty made it unnecessary for me to answer. He said, "Wait until Christine finds out what she missed!"

"That's what she gets for being such a rotten person inside," said Brenda Belle.

Everyone began circling around Billie Kay, including Ty and Brenda Belle. There were about twenty people at the party, kids from school and some of their parents, none of them particular friends of mine or my grandfather's.

Billie Kay was in her glory. Rufus Kerin asked her for her autograph, which started the ball rolling. Everyone was getting out pieces of paper and pens and pencils.

I looked around for my grandfather, but he wasn't anywhere in view. I went back into the kitchen to see if he was there, and he wasn't. I paused in front of the telephone. I was thinking of Christine and Nothing Power. I picked up the Storm telephone directory and began running my finger down the column of C's. Then I dialed.

A man answered and I asked to speak to her.

"Who's calling?" he said.

"Adam," I said.

"Adam?" he said.

"Adam Blessing," I said.

"Oh."

"Is Christine there?" I said.

"What is it you want?" he said.

"I want to wish Christine a happy New Year, that's all," I said.

He said, "I'll give her the message."

Then he hung up.

I felt as though I'd been slapped across the mouth suddenly, for no reason, by a stranger. I thought of the postcard Brenda Belle and I had sent to him, to make him feel more appreciated. I mean, he could have said, "And a happy New Year to you," or something; he could have at least said good-bye before he hung up. Nothing Power hadn't done much to improve his personality. . . . At least Rufus Kerin had shown its effects—at least Rufus had appeared with a smile, wearing a new suit, looking a lot different than he looked driving that bus and snarling at us kids.

I found my grandfather sitting in his bedroom, sipping coffee. Janice was on his lap.

"She's scared of all the people," he said while he petted her.

"Billie Kay's told everyone who she is."

"I heard."

"I guess she won't give me away though," I said. I sat down on the bed. I couldn't help wishing that Billie Kay would give me away. It had something to do with Ty Hardin's cracks about our glasses and the tree; Brenda Belle's fussing over him; and Dr. Cutler's abrupt manner on the telephone. I remembered a report one of the schools once sent to my father concerning my progress, or lack of it. *Adam is too self-conscious of the fact he is your son. This is a major detriment to his own personality development.*

My grandfather said, "Go back and join the party, A.J. You don't have to keep me company."

"Maybe I want *your* company," I said.

"I'm not much company without a glass in my hand. I don't have much to say."

"I don't, either," I said. "Do you think I have much personality, Grandpa?"

"You're doing fine, A.J. You haven't been here a month, and you have a girlfriend already."

"I don't know that she's really interested in me," I said.

"Are you that interested in her?" he said.

"I just don't know," I sighed. I couldn't bring myself to mention Christine Cutler. If she'd been anyone but a Cutler, I would have liked to discuss her with my grandfather. I said, "Brenda Belle is a nice girl, but I don't know if we should be going steady. It sort of limits us. It's very important to her to go steady, because of her mother."

"It's tough for a girl like Brenda Belle," said my grandfather. "She lives with those two old-maid types, no man around the place. Her mother was old-fashioned even in her own time. She should have lived back when Christmas was banned in New England—those times suit her better."

"I know," I said. "I'm sorry for Brenda Belle."

"I told you once before, don't make that mistake," said my grandfather. "When you pity someone, sometimes all that means is you wish someone would pity you."

Suddenly there was a lot of noise from the other room. People were blowing the horns Billie Kay had bought, and beginning to count down from ten.

"Get back to the party, A.J.!" my grandfather said. "It's almost midnight!"

"Happy New Year, Grandpa!"

"Same to you, A.J.!"

I ran toward the living room so I wouldn't disappoint Brenda Belle on the stroke of midnight.

Marlon Fredenberg, the football hero, was taking pictures with his new Polaroid.

"Three . . . Two . . ." Billie Kay was counting.

"Where's Brenda Belle?" I asked Marlon.

"One! . . . Happy New Year!" Billie Kay shouted.

Marlon glanced down at me with this lopsided grin. "They're gone," he said. "They took off in Ty's car."

Someone began a chorus of "Auld Lang Syne."

Notes for a Novel by B.B.B.

When Ty Hardin said, "Let's get out of here!" I
was glad to go. It wasn't particularly because I
wanted to be alone with Tyrone Hardin—the idea
of me being alone with someone like Tyrone Hardin
wasn't even real to me. What was real was overhearing Adam calling Christine Cutler in the kitchen
when I'd gone back there to get him prepared for
our midnight kiss. He'd seemed mad at me over
something, and I'd headed back to get it straightened
out before the New Year was rung in. I was practically in tears after I heard him ask for Christine.
It seemed like a fantastic stroke of luck to suddenly
have the alternative of sweeping out the door with
Christine's steady boyfriend.

The reality of my situation didn't begin to sink

in until we were headed along Ski Tow Avenue in Ty's father's white Cougar. He snapped on the car radio, and as "Auld Lang Syne" was playing, he put his arm around me and drew me close to him.

"Happy New Year," he said, kissing my cheek.

"Be careful," I said. "I didn't plan to die this year."

He turned up the radio and stepped down on the gas pedal. I thought to myself maybe death was preferable to trying to think of the right thing to say to someone like Tyrone Hardin. What was I even doing with Tyrone Hardin?

I studied his profile to see if there was any drastic change in his facial expression, any winces or sudden tics. Outwardly he didn't seem to be affected by the fact he had Brenda Belle Blossom with him, when he could have had just about any girl in Storm.

The thing about being with someone like Ty is that you immediately think about how you look, and if you've always been bugged about how you look, you become twice as bugged. I doubt that this happens to males in the same way it happens to females. In the movies there are always instances of not-so-great-looking males involved with fantastic-looking females, but it is hard to recall a movie where a not-so-great-looking female is being pursued by a fantastic-looking male. Maybe that's because males make the movies, I don't know.

112

I do know that I rode along beside him thinking: "He is *beautiful*!" and everything I'd learned about male/female relationships at my mother's knee told me there was something wrong about that. The male is supposed to be thinking that; the female is supposed to be thinking: I'm glad I am so beautiful that he wants to be with me. At least that's the way it appeared to me, in all my vast, unliberated knowledge of the sexes.

Every part of my body was locked in tight except my mouth. I could always depend on my mouth. It had a life of its own, and it was determined to live it.

"Where are we heading at such a snail's pace?" I said, holding on as we squealed around a turn.

"I thought I was taking you home."

"There's no one there."

"That's why I thought we were going there."

"Help! Police! Rape!" I shouted.

Ty laughed. "Is that what you're planning?"

"If you'll hold still long enough," my mouth said, but I wasn't laughing. I was sitting there shivering and wondering what my mouth was getting me into.

"Listen to this song," Ty said. "I like this song."

I listened long enough to hear the words and take in the fact it was a very sentimental song. I tried to picture Christine Cutler in my place, and to fathom what she'd answer. What? *Beautiful, Ty*, in her most moving dulcet tones. *Oh, Ty, how very lovely*.

"Kiss, bliss, miss," I said. "Isn't it nice that everything rhymes?"

"Don't you like that song, Brenda B.?" he said.

"Last night, held me tight, see the light," I said. "How veddy veddy original."

Before I knew it, Ty had stopped the car. He hadn't pulled over to the side of the road, or said anything; he had simply braked, slipped into neutral, and stopped.

"What's the matter?" I said.

I got a fast look at his face, just long enough to see that he wasn't smiling. Then I felt a beard along my cheeks, and his lips pressed against mine, and his arms around me. I remember I began by thinking: He has a beard (!), because he was so fair-haired I hadn't noticed that about him; and then I thought: His hair tickles, because it was almost as long as my hair. . . . Then I didn't think, or I don't remember what I thought, because I began to feel something completely unfamiliar, this floating sensation, this nice limbo.

The next thing I knew he was just looking at me while he took a cigarette from his coat pocket and lighted it, all of this with the same hand. His other arm was around my shoulder. His eyes were trying to fix on mine, but I just stared at his necktie.

My mouth finally surfaced for breath and asserted itself. "Warning," it said with great effort. "The

114

Surgeon General has determined that cigarette smoking is dangerous to your health."

I had never heard my poor mouth sound so beaten down.

Ty sensed the difference, smiled, and chucked me under the chin.

Then he started the car going again. He said, "You're right at the top of the hill, aren't you?"

"Yes. We live there," I managed.

"Want a cigarette?" he said, offering me the pack.

I took one, although I didn't smoke. "Why let the Surgeon General run your affairs?" I said, wishing I hadn't chosen the word "affair."

Ty snapped his lighter and I leaned forward to light my cigarette.

I drew in and coughed.

"Do you think you're going to enjoy smoking?" he said.

"Nobody lives forever," I answered. My hands were shaking. I sat on the left one, and kept the right one, with the cigarette between my fingers, close to me.

Ty parked out in front, but he didn't get out of the car after he stopped it. He turned to me again and I drifted into him and we stayed in the front seat for quite a long time.

"Do you want to go inside?" he finally said, lighting another cigarette for me.

I felt as though I'd been punched by feathers or socked with some invisible force which rocked my psyche but left the rest of me intact. I could move, anyway; I could go through the motions: walk, talk. "Come on in," I said. I opened the car door and felt a wave of cold air hit my face. It revived my mouth. "I'll show you my etchings," I said. For some reason, I began to walk ahead of him, very fast, as though it was a matter of life and death that I get to the front door before he did. I opened the door and walked in, left the door open and didn't wait for him to catch up. I called over my shoulder, "Momento while I drink a bottle of iodine in the bathroom."

I headed upstairs, into the hall bathroom, with my coat still on and the burning cigarette still held between my fingers like it was in a vise.

I shut the door, and leaned against it for strength, and looked at my reflection across the way in the mirror of the medicine cabinet.

"Well, dearie," I said to it, "what in the hell is happening here?"

Then I tossed my cigarette into the toilet, flushed, and tried to work my coat buttons like any normal person.

My mother always leaves the overhead light on in the living room when we're not home evenings. (We're not home evenings about three evenings a year.) She does this on the theory that burglars expect lamps to be on, but not overhead lights. Our house has never been burgled: I can't recall ever hearing of a thief entering anyone's house in Storm. Furthermore, my mother never locks the doors, but that is beside the point.

The point is that when I came back downstairs, the overhead light was off, and a small table lamp was on. Ty was sitting on the couch, dropping his cigarette ashes into a Kleenex.

"Do you have an ashtray?" he said.

"I'll get a saucer from the kitchen," I said. "Do you want a Coke?"

"On New Year's Eve?" he laughed.

"There's nothing here," I said, "but some sweet sherry my aunt takes for her arthritis."

"Then we'll just have to make do," Ty said. "Sherry it is."

"If you hear my mother drive up," I said, "hide the glass. If you don't hear her drive up, and she drives up, prepare to die."

I went into the kitchen for the saucer and a tumbler of sherry. I opened a Coke for myself. I'd already had two glasses of punch.

After I poured Ty's drink, the sherry bottle was almost empty. I diluted what was left with water and put it back in place on the cupboard, behind the box of shredded wheat.

In the living room our radio was playing, and Ty was sitting sideways on the couch, with one arm drawn over the back of it.

I handed him the tumbler of sherry, ignored the fact that he patted the cushion next to him as a gesture for me to sit down there, and crossed the room to the armchair.

"What's the matter?" he said.

"Nothing is," I said, but something *was* the matter with carrying on, the way we had in the car, there in the very living room where my mother and aunt spent nearly every evening of their lives.

"I suppose you miss Adam," he said.

"Adam who?" my mouth took over.

"Do you let Adam kiss you the way I kissed you?"

"Do you let Christine kiss you the way I kissed you?" There was something radically wrong with that answer, or unfeminine, as my mother would say . . . something not right; but I had to take things as they came, since protocol wasn't exactly dominating the ambiance.

"Christine and I have broken up," he said. "Sit over here."

"Why?" I said.

"I don't like you to be far away."

"I mean why have you broken up?"

"Why aren't *you* with Adam?" he said. "You're supposed to be going steady."

"No comment," I said, "under advice of my lawyers."

"What do you know about him?" he said, taking a swig of the sherry. He winced. "This is really sweet!"

"Sweets for the sweet," I said. "I know things about him that nobody knows." But I had no intention of telling Ty that Adam had been kicked out of private school for cheating.

"Is he a joker?" Ty asked.

"He's very serious."

"Christine says he's not a joker, either."

"What does Christine Cutler know about Adam?" I said angrily.

"She just said he wasn't the type to send this postcard to her father," Ty said. "Her father got this strange postcard in the mail, something about leaving someone behind him."

"He must have left someone behind him," I said, playing it very cool. "What would Adam send a postcard like that to Dr. Cutler for?"

"Search me," Ty said, "but Dr. Cutler's got it in his head that Adam might have done it."

"Ridic!" I said. "Ridic and prepost! Adam doesn't even know him."

"I know, I know," Ty said. "I guess he blames Adam because Adam is new in town."

"*Blames* Adam? Didn't he like the postcard?"

"No, he didn't. He said some prankster sent it."

"Adam isn't the type. Adam lived right next door to Billie Kay Case at one time and he's very worldly."

"He doesn't act it. He had some nerve saying he wouldn't go to Christine's party because it'd bore him." Ty took another swig of sherry. "That really got to Christine. She couldn't get over it."

"Christine Cutlers are a dime a dozen to someone like Adam," I said.

"He's nothing," said Ty.

"There is such a thing as Nothing Power," I said.

Ty gave a snort. "Well, that's exactly what he's got: Nothing Power."

"And Dr. Cutler is a big jackass if he thinks Adam would mail him any kind of postcard."

"I don't know how he got that notion into his head, either," said Ty. "I guess it's because Adam's new and Christine's been talking about him a lot. Also, Doc Cutler hates anyone with the name Blessing."

I said, "Christine's been talking about him a lot?"

He patted the cushion next to him. "Come on over and see me," he said.

I said, "Christine Cutler has been talking about Adam Blessing a lot?"

"Enough to make me think she's had a lobotomy performed," Ty snickered. "Her wires are crossed."

"Is that what you fought about?" I said.

120

"Come over here and sit beside me, Brenda B.," he said.

"Is that what you fought about?" I said.

"That's the last thing I'd fight about," said Ty. "Do you think I'd take someone like him for serious competition?"

"If you insult him, you insult me," I said. "We're going steady."

Ty laughed aloud.

"We *are*!" I insisted. "We just had a slight lover's quarrel tonight."

"If you won't come to me, I'll come to you," Ty said. He stood up and came across the room.

I managed to say, "Is this the way you treat Christine?" before he sat down on the hassock by my feet and pulled me toward him.

"I don't care about Christine," he said, while his lips brushed my cheek very lightly. "I care about you."

I could feel my mouth fading into the background, leaving just me to handle things. Just me is a very weak entity, practically a nonentity.

"I care about you," Ty said again.

"You do?" I whispered.

"I really do."

"I'm going steady," I said.

"I know," he said.

"This isn't right," I said.

121

"It's right," he said. "What feels right is right."

"Not always," I said.

"Always," he said.

"Brenda Belle?" my mother said. "Brenda Belle?"

I jumped to my feet, nearly knocking Ty over. "Mother?" I called back. I whispered to Ty, "The sherry!"

I yelled, "We're in here, Mother," and I dashed across and turned on the overhead light. Ty grabbed his overcoat and stuck the half-full tumbler of sherry in his pocket. Then he put the coat carefully over his arm.

"Why did you leave the party?" my mother said as she came into the living room. "Hello, Ty."

"Hello, Mrs. Blossom," he said, and then he said, "I'm afraid it's all my fault Brenda Belle left the party early. You see, I didn't like the way Adam was treating Brenda Belle."

My Aunt Faith followed my mother into the living room.

"What do you mean?" said my mother.

"I mean you don't just ignore a lady, not on New Year's Eve."

"Oh, that was Billie Kay's fault," my Aunt Faith said. "She was causing a lot of excitement, and I think—"

But my mother didn't let my aunt finish. Ty had said the magic word: "Lady."

"That was very considerate of you, Ty," said my mother. "What happened to Christine tonight?"

"Christine didn't feel well," said Ty. "Thank you for asking. I guess I'd better be getting along."

As he picked up his cigarettes, he managed to wipe up the ring left by the tumbler of sherry. He slipped the piece of Kleenex up his shirt sleeve. My mother and my aunt didn't notice. They didn't notice anything strange about the slow way he moved across the room, either, being certain not to disturb the half-full tumbler in his overcoat pocket.

I followed him to the door.

He whispered at me, "What feels right is right."

Then in a loud voice he said, "I'll see you, Brenda Belle! Tell Adam he'd better brush up his manners if he wants to keep you! Good night! Happy New Year!"

I felt like my legs had turned to rubber. I was definitely not immune to Tyrone Hardin. I felt as though I'd had a heart transplant, only a drum had been put inside to replace the heart.

As soon as I shut the door, my mother said, "Brenda Belle, what kind of a lady *are* you? You got yourself a Coke, but you didn't give him anything. Didn't he want anything?"

Before I could defend myself she said, "If a gentleman doesn't want anything when a lady offers him something, then a lady doesn't have anything, either."

123

"I had such a nice time!" my Aunt Faith said.

"Fawning over that boisterous woman!" said my mother. "I was embarrassed for you, Faith."

"Were you, Millie?" my aunt said. "What a pity you couldn't enjoy yourself."

"I don't think much of Adam Blessing *or* that Christmas tree tied with beer cans," said my mother. "I didn't expect anything from old Charlie, but Brenda Belle, you led me to believe his grandson was a nice boy."

"He *is* a nice boy, Millie," my aunt said.

"You heard what the Hardin boy said about him, Faith," my mother said. "The *Hardin* boy is a nice boy. He's a gentleman. He called Brenda Belle a lady."

"Does that automatically make me a lady?" I said.

"In his eyes, I would say so," said my mother.

"And I would say *so what!*" said my aunt, yawning.

"Nighty-night, all," I said. "Don't enjoy yourselves too much."

"I don't intend to enjoy myself at all," said my mother, marching upstairs behind me.

From the Journal of A.

After Brenda Belle left the party with Ty Hardin, I made a jackass of myself by drinking too much punch. I even threw up. My father is fond of saying that the second most disgusting thing is a throw-up drunk. (The first most disgusting thing, according to him, is a beggar. "If you ever find yourself on your knees, A.J.," he is also fond of saying, "don't beg. Pray!")

I don't think I was really jealous of Ty Hardin, or anything like that. I was just tired of trying to please people and not being able to, and trying to behave as someone thought I should, and discovering it didn't make any difference, anyway.

I suppose the reason Brenda Belle didn't wait for our first kiss at the stroke of midnight was that she

125

began to see me and my grandfather through Ty Hardin's eyes. The beer cans on the tree and the jelly glasses probably got to her, and she just took off with him—the hell with Nothing Power and the fact we were supposed to be going steady. I was also still smarting from the very perfunctory way I'd been treated by Dr. Cutler when I'd called Christine. . . . I guess I felt like a jackass and that's why I turned into one.

I fell asleep next to Janice atop some pillows on the floor of my grandfather's bedroom. Billie Kay had passed out on the living-room couch, which was where I was supposed to sleep.

When I woke up, I had such a bad headache I couldn't move right away. I heard my grandfather's side of a conversation with one of his sons (an uncle I had never met) who had made one of his rare telephone calls in honor of the new year. My grandfather's sons were not exactly the attentive types, and my grandfather's conversation with the only one who'd called during the holidays was subdued and short. ("I'm having a wonderful time," he said, "so don't worry about me. I've got Annabell's boy here and we're getting to know each other, so don't worry about me at all.")

After he hung up, he and Billie Kay began talking together in the living room . . . if you could call it talking *together*. My grandfather was talking about my mother, and Billie Kay was talking about my father and Billie Kay.

I stared up at the ceiling and listened for a while.

"He never told me anything about Annabell," Billie Kay was saying. "What was she like? He never liked to discuss his past. I told him everything from apples to zucchini about my life, but Mr. Big Deal liked to live in the present."

My grandfather said, "She was just another young girl, very young, small town. Her mother died giving her life, and I raised her by myself. When she was little she said she wanted to be a vet like me. I would have liked that. I wasn't close to my boys. None of my boys wanted to follow in my footsteps."

"I once wanted to be an architect," said Billie Kay. "A builder of bridges. I became a burner of bridges behind me, instead."

"About a year before it was time for her to go to college, I hired a young assistant. Cutler. He was a married student over at the university, and he needed the job."

"Yes, I've burned plenty of bridges behind me in my time," Billie Kay said, "and I've crossed plenty of bridges before I came to them."

My grandfather said, "For a while she helped us out. Then she went to New York City, skipped the whole idea of going to college—just took off."

"He never told me about his years in New York City," Billie Kay said. (He never told me, either.)

My grandfather said, "She met him there and married him less than a month later. I only met him once. At her funeral."

"For all I know about your past, I used to tell him, you're from Mars or Venus. More likely Venus." Billie Kay laughed.

"He was all in pieces," my grandfather said.

"I'm in pieces right now," Billie Kay said. "I've got three thousand little men with hammers buried under my skin, and they're all beating on my bones. Two thousand nine hundred of them are located inside my head."

"I'll make some more coffee," my grandfather said.

I was trying to picture my father all in pieces. I'd seen him drunk, and I'd seen him depressed, but he was always all in one piece and tough as a chuck roast. If he was ever down, his hands were always balled in fists, and he never stayed down very long.

I was also letting the new accord between Billie Kay and my grandfather register. They were actually carrying on a conversation of sorts; at least they weren't taking swipes at each other. I didn't know how that had evolved, but one of the last things I remembered about the party was that my grandfather began taking charge toward the end of the evening.

He was getting food into people who were driving, and he was emptying ashtrays. He was being very gentle with Billie Kay, too. She was sitting around with her head practically hanging between her knees, and her cigarettes almost burning off the skin on her fingers. She was complaining about not getting any residuals from her old movies being shown on television. My grandfather was saying things like, "Well, you got a right to be mad about that, they *should* pay you," and "No, you're not boring me, that's quite all right."

I hadn't ever seen my grandfather in that role before. Usually at the end of the evening, he was the hang-head and the complainer. He'd also stuck to his bargain, which surprised me a little, and he hadn't said anything when Billie Kay didn't stick to hers and tried to catch Janice to give her "a big Moo Year's smooch." (Janice hid behind the shower curtain in the bathroom until the moment passed.)

Someday I hope some adult will explain to me what's so damned funny about having a hangover. Why does a hangover always get a laugh? Both Billie Kay and my grandfather thought it was a huge joke when I came out of the bedroom with my bloodshot eyes, holding my head with my hands.

"Welcome to the club," Billie Kay said. "Oh, A.J., are *you* a beautiful sight!"

My grandfather stood in the kitchen doorway chuckling.

"Is this your generation's idea of having a good time?" I said.

"I suppose you kids have a better idea," Billie Kay said. "Like shooting up until you become welfare cases."

"I've got a pot of black-eyed peas cooking," my grandfather said, "made Southern style with salt pork and corn pone to soak up the pot liquor. You know," he began, "if you eat black-eyed peas on New Year's Day, you have good luck all year. That superstition dates back to—"

Never mind the rest. My grandfather was his old self again.

By the time I had begun to recover from my hangover several hours later, Billie Kay and my grandfather were talking about a franchise business called Ice Cream Boats. Billie Kay was telling him this chain was mushrooming on the west coast, and that he ought to get into something just like it. My grandfather was protesting that he was too old, sounding younger by the minute.

I decided to go for a walk. I knew where I was going as I put on my coat. I'd known since the night before when I'd begun drowning my sorrow in the punch bowl. I wasn't admitting it right out to myself, but my feet knew where I was going, and they took me straight there, down Ski Tow Avenue, up Rider Road and through the woods to Herman Avenue.

It was a balmy afternoon for winter in Vermont. The sun was out and there was a certain mildness to the weather that reminded me of January in Virginia. My father had a house in Virginia during his first years in Washington. It was smack in the middle of the Shenandoah Valley, and I used to love that house —until I discovered that most of the time I was the only one home, unless you want to count the housekeeper.

I used to think that after I got married and began to raise a family, I'd live in Virginia. That was when I was about nine years old, before I realized what a complicated idea getting married was, and before I appreciated the fact you can't just plunk yourself down in any state you want to and live there: You have to do something for a living. I gave up the plan as soon as I was aware there were all those strings attached. The best way was not to have any plans, just glide. I was the glider type.

But that afternoon while I was walking along, I thought of living in Virginia again. I was humming that old folk song, "Oh, Shenandoah, I long to see you," going along trying to ignore where I was going, at the same time talking myself into it.

I figured the worst that could happen was that she'd just slam the door in my face. I hadn't done anything to deserve having the door slammed in my face, so it probably wouldn't happen. I figured, too, that she might welcome some interest on anyone's part, because of being ditched on New Year's Eve. . . . I knew I'd welcome some interest on someone's part. I'd been ditched, too.

When I got to her house, I almost walked past it. Then I decided that if nothing else, an explanation was due me as to why she hadn't wanted Brenda Belle to bring me to her Christmas Eve party.

I pictured my father in the same situation. I squared my shoulders and stuck out my jaw (which wasn't my father's style at all) and then I let my muscles relax and let my face soften, and thought of this gentle facade camouflaging this steel trap (which *was* my father's style when he was wheeling and dealing) . . . and I went forward.

The doorbell rang chimes.

"Hello, Christine," I said. "Happy New Year."

She said, "Adam, you should have called before you came here."

I said, "I called last night."

"I know," she said. She was all in black: black pants, black sweater, with her blonde hair spilling past her shoulders, and she kept looking behind her nervously.

I said, "Happy New Year."

"Happy New Year," she finally said. "I don't think you'd better come in."

132

"Then come out," I said. "Come for a walk."

A man appeared behind her. He was a pipe smoker like my grandfather. I took this as a good sign.

He was a medium-height, balding, bespectacled man. I couldn't fathom him stealing anyone's business out from under him, much less ever being involved in revolting and repulsive things. He had soft eyes and a pleasant, boyish grin.

"This is my father," Christine said.

I said, "How do you do, sir?"

"Hi," he said.

Christine said, "Daddy, this is Adam Blessing."

He didn't say anything right away and I just stood there for a moment trying to figure out what had come over him. The only way I can describe it is that it was as though he'd come to the door in a perfectly pleasant frame of mind and suddenly discovered something all wrong with what was standing there on his doorstep. He didn't seem angry. The word was: unwilling.

I was surprised by my own voice blurting out, "I don't know anything about what went on between my grandfather and you. I just wanted to wish Christine a Happy New Year."

He cleared his throat. He gave me a certain look, the kind that says you're expendable, like the contagious person in the crowded lifeboat or the fat man at the famine.

"Don't be long, Christine," he said. Then he disappeared from view.

"Christine, what's the matter?" I said.

"Nothing is," she said.

"*Something* is."

"Let me get my coat," she said.

She closed the door and I stood there for what seemed like a very long time. I wished I'd never gone there; I wanted to glide back into the scenery.

Then she appeared wearing this fur-collared coat around her shoulders, and when I tried to help her put it on, she said, "No, I'm not going to be out here long."

"We could go for a walk," I said.

"No, we can't," she said. "Anyway, wouldn't a walk bore you?"

"What are you talking about, Christine?"

"If my Christmas Eve party would bore you, wouldn't a walk bore you?"

"You didn't even ask me to your party," I said.

"I asked Brenda Belle to ask you and she said you said it would bore you."

"Brenda Belle said you told her not to bring me," I said.

"I only asked her because I wanted you to come," she said.

"She didn't tell me that," I said.

"She said you said it would bore you."

134

"I never said that," I said.

"Anyway, it doesn't matter," she said.

"It matters," I said. "Of course it matters. Why are we standing here like this? Come for a walk."

"I can't," she said. "Did you send my father a strange card?"

"No," I said.

"He thinks you did."

"Is that why he acts that way?" I said.

"He doesn't like you, Adam."

"He doesn't even know me."

"He says he doesn't know anything about you."

"Then how can he dislike me?"

"He says you're an unknown quantity."

"How can he dislike an unknown quantity?"

"It goes back to the thing with Charlie," she said.

"Don't call my grandfather Charlie," I said.

"Everyone in Storm calls him Charlie," she said.

"Do you like me?"

"What?"

"You heard me."

She said, "My father is watching us."

"He can't read lips, can he?"

"I like you all right," she said.

"I like you, too."

"This is awful," she said.

"What's awful about liking each other? I liked you from the moment I saw you."

"You don't know my father."

"How can he dislike an unknown quantity?"

"It goes back to the thing with your grandfather."

"What happened, what exactly happened?"

"I don't know," she said.

The front door opened and her father called out, "Christine?"

Christine called back, "Okay, Daddy, I'm coming."

"I'll see you in school," I said.

"You're going steady with Brenda Belle," she said.

"I can explain that."

"Don't bother. It won't make any difference."

"I'll see you in school," I said.

"It won't do any good," she said. "You're an unknown quantity."

"How can you dislike an unknown quantity?"

"*I* don't, Adam!"

Her father's voice again, "CHRISTINE!"

She said, "I'll see you in school."

"I'll see you," I said.

"See you," she said, and she went back up the walk and inside the house.

That night when Brenda Belle called to announce she'd run off because she'd overheard me trying to call Christine, I didn't tell her about going there that afternoon. I was tempted to really yell at her for lying about Christine's Christmas Eve party, but I was too high from seeing Christine to be mad at anyone.

Brenda Belle said, "I forgive you if you forgive me."

"I forgive everyone," I said, "for everything."

"That's wonderful, sweetheart," she said. "Besides, he didn't even call me today."

"Who didn't call you today?"

"Ty Hardin," she said. "He didn't even call me."

Then she said, "Adam? I want to read you something my aunt found in Helen Stiles' 'Stars Today' column. It's all about Billie Kay's ex!"

This is what she read to me:

The powerful bigwig seen around Tinsel Town with Electric Socket was rumored to be mucho involved at Washington's Sans Souci restaurant with the widow of you-know-who. Is there a short circuit in Electric's socket, or was Mr. Powerful just whispering state secrets into Widow Wonderful's ears?

"That's wonderful, sweetheart," I said. "A million thanks for sharing it with me."

Notes for a Novel by B.B.B.

Groundhog Day is a late date for making New Year's resolutions, but I made one then, anyway.

My resolution was to try and stop being a sneak. It was inspired by a conversation I overheard between my mother and my aunt as I was dressing for school.

They were in my mother's room, where my mother was getting ready for her once-a-month trip to the Burlington Shopping Center.

"Even though I don't approve of your drinking," my mother was saying, "I would not water down your sherry, Faith."

"My *drinking*?" my aunt said. "Just how much do you think I drink? I've had that bottle of Dry Sack since last September!"

"That's your own business," said my mother.

"I hope to tell you!" my aunt said. "And I hope to tell you I know the difference between sherry with water added to it and undiluted sherry!"

"I'm sure you know a great deal about alcohol," my mother said. "My ignorance on the subject is well known—so well known that I married an alcoholic without even being aware what he was."

"Hank was not an alcoholic, Millie!"

"*You* weren't his wife, Faith. His sidekick, maybe; his *buddy*, indeed . . . but not his wife."

"I know what he wasn't. I didn't have to be his wife to know what he wasn't."

"You knew what he wasn't, and I knew what he was," said my mother. "I don't want to get on *that* subject. You have more trouble forgetting him than I do."

My aunt said, "I wouldn't be proud of the fact I could so easily forget the man I married."

"*You* married Doc Hendricks, Faith."

"I haven't forgotten that, and I haven't forgotten Doc."

"We both know you remember Hank better, but I don't want to get on *that* subject."

"No. Please, *don't*," said my aunt.

"Don't worry, Faith, I won't. I'd like to forget the way you made such a fool of yourself, laughing like a loon around him, thinking you enjoyed some special intimacy with him because he treated you like one of the boys. Well, a man doesn't marry one of the boys!"

I heard my aunt slam the door and hurry down the stairs.

When my mother stopped by my room to ask if she could drop me at school, I told her I wasn't ready, that I'd take the bus.

After she left, I went downstairs where my aunt was sipping tea and watching a morning television show.

I said, "Aunt Faith, may I say something?"

"Of course, dear." I knew that she'd been crying.

"*I* watered down the sherry," I said. Then I told her about giving Ty Hardin a tumbler of it on New Year's Eve. I told her a lot of things I hadn't told anyone, not even Adam. I told her everything that had happened between Ty and me after we left the party, and I told her how Ty was behaving toward me as though none of it had ever happened, as though I was just this character he swatted across the back and traded quips with. Then I told her about Nothing Power.

"None of it worked," I said. "It didn't change anything or anyone, and Adam and I are just these two phonies pretending to be going steady."

"Is it Ty Hardin you really care for?" she asked.

"I don't even know," I said. "I only know I feel

differently about him than I do about Adam. And I think Adam feels that way about Christine Cutler."

"Brenda Belle," she said, "Nothing Power was a nice idea but you can't play God. You can't make someone feel like something unless you really mean it . . . any more than you can decide to go steady with someone unless you both really feel it."

"I thought it would make Mother happy," I said.

"I know," my aunt said, "but you can't see the world through your mother's glasses. You'll just see a distortion."

"She really does have a distorted viewpoint!" I said emphatically.

"No, I didn't mean that," my aunt said. "She sees things her way, and that's right for her. It's like a prescription for eyeglasses. You can't use someone else's."

"But there has to be a right way to look at things!" I said.

"There simply isn't one way, Brenda Belle. The right way is what you grow to learn is right for you. All your life you'll find people who differ with you, who don't see things as you do. From time to time you'll change your own way of seeing things, too."

"I don't care about the future," I said. "I just want to get through right now."

"Then don't hurry yourself into the future," my

aunt said. "Don't force it. It'll be here fast enough."

"Thanks, Aunt Faith," I said, "I'm going to think about it hard."

"Don't think about it too hard," she said. "Relax . . . and about Ty Hardin, honey, just be yourself around him. If he's pretending New Year's Eve didn't happen, that only means he's having trouble being *himself*. Everybody has trouble finding his way, remember that—you're not the only one."

"I'm sorry I didn't tell you about the sherry before this," I said.

"I forgive you this time," said my aunt, "but always remember two things. Own up to sparks before they're fires, and never serve sherry in a tall glass."

While I waited for the bus that morning I tried to concentrate on my English assignment. We were supposed to memorize some short poetry that expressed poignancy. I'd found one written by someone named Frances Cornford, called "To a Fat Lady Seen from the Train."

This is it:

> O why do you walk through the fields in gloves,
>   Missing so much and so much?
> O fat white woman whom nobody loves,
> Why do you walk through the fields in gloves
> When the grass is as soft as the breast of doves
> And shivering-sweet to the touch?

142

The poem took on a whole new meaning after that talk with my aunt. It wasn't so much what we'd talked about; it was more the difference between my aunt and my mother. I'd always thought my mother was just plain mean a lot of the time, and I still don't think she'll ever be handed any bouquets for kindness. But in a way it was as though life was that field in the poem, and my mother was going through it wearing gloves, while my aunt was going through it with her gloves off. From my mother's point of view, life was just going along, maybe being aware of what was around her, but never allowing herself to touch it . . . maybe because she was afraid to soil her hands, maybe because it just never occurred to her to reach out. But my aunt reached out, put more into living, and got more back: that's why she wasn't mean.

I think I understood something else about my mother that morning, too. The reason she didn't like the fact I was like my aunt wasn't at all because she thought my aunt was a failure as a woman. It was really because she was jealous of my aunt. She couldn't bear the idea that growing up in that house with the two of them, I'd followed my aunt's example instead of hers. . . . She made so much of the fact she was the woman my father had married, but it was my aunt my father had laughed with, and my aunt who'd understood him . . . and she made so much of the fact she had a daughter, but it was my aunt I emulated, and my aunt who understood me.

If it wasn't a very pretty picture, it was a clearer picture of my mother and me than I'd ever had before. The new light I saw her in didn't make me dislike her, but I had the distinct feeling she wasn't going to get to me again, as she had in the past.

When the bus rolled toward me, I made that New Year's resolution about trying not to be such a sneak. Honesty had paid off with my Aunt Faith. I decided there was something else I had to take care of—this business of Adam and me going steady. We had to call off the whole thing. I had his ring in my pocket, ready to return it.

Something was happening to Adam. He was moody, and he had become this terrible show-off. He was also beginning to flunk tests he should have passed with flying colors.

Rufus Kerin was driving the bus, and as I climbed aboard he looked right through me when I said hello. The only thing changed about Rufus Kerin was his dashboard. Scotch-taped to it was Billie Kay Case's autograph. Otherwise he was the same grouchy Rufus he'd been before the establishment of Nothing Power.

As far as I could tell, there'd been no change in Dr. Cutler, Marilyn Pepper or Ella Early, either.

So much for Nothing Power, I thought, and I looked for Adam when the bus reached the bottom of the hill. He wasn't there. The week before he'd over-slept twice, arriving at school midway through English.

That was another symptom of his change: he was late a lot for everything.

I guess the strangest happening was his flunking the history test. Mouse Meredith teaches History, and his idea of history is names, places and dates. Old Mighty Mouse doesn't care why we fought the Civil War; he only cares where and when we fought it. He's the same way about everything, from the Boston Tea Party to Paul Revere's ride.

Adam had predicted that Mighty Mouse would ask for the names of all the United States presidents, and that he'd want them listed in order. Then Adam had devised this neat way for us to remember the information. To give you an example, take these sentences.

WE ARE JUST MAKING MORE QUINCE-APPLE JAM. VAN HAS TYPED PAUL THAT FIG PIES BAKE LOVELY.

There you have all the presidents through Lincoln, in order, with clues like MA for Madison, MO for Monroe, QUINCEAPPLE for John Quincy Adams (as distinguished from John Adams), TY for Tyler (as distinguished from Taylor) and PI for Pierce (as distinguished from Polk).

After you have memorized the sentences, it is

145

practically impossible to ever forget. . . . But Adam, who had invented the whole system and taught it to me, blocked on test day. He had to hand Mouse a blank test book.

When the bus arrived at school, I was surprised to see Adam waiting to meet it.

"I got a phone call early this morning," he explained to me. "I couldn't sleep after, so I got dressed and walked around town. I just ended up here, about an hour ago."

"Did Billie Kay call you?" I said.

"She isn't the *only* person I know who'd call me," he said. "I do have a father."

"How is he?" I said. I couldn't picture his father. I had some hazy image of this shoe salesman, this man going around with his sample cases, like that actor, Frederick March, in the old movie *Death of a Salesman*.

I'd been wishing it'd been Billie Kay who'd called him, because anything and everything about her fascinated me. She was the only real live celebrity I'd ever met.

Adam shrugged. "He's okay, I guess."

Adam had told me that his mother was dead, but he'd never told me much about either of his parents. I thought that his father was some kind of failure, someone Adam wasn't very proud of.

"He sort of wants me to show up for something

146

in a few weeks," he said. "I may have to go out there."

"Go out where?"

"The coast."

"Then you'll see Billie Kay. Will you? Will you see Billie Kay?"

"I suppose I'll see her. Grandpa may come with me."

"Will you ask her when she's doing that special? She said she was going to make a special for television."

"A lot of things she says she's going to do don't pan out," he said.

"Ask her anyway."

"I don't really want to go."

"Do you have to go?"

"Yes, I have to go."

We were about to approach The Pillars. They're right in front of the school entrance, and that's where everyone hangs around before first bell.

I felt Adam's arm around my shoulder.

I wasn't surprised, but I knew, by then, what it meant.

It meant Christine Cutler was one of the people hanging around The Pillars. It meant Adam was going to act real turned on to me.

"Show time," I said sarcastically. "Curtain up."

Adam didn't pick up on the sarcasm. He was

147

pulling me closer and looking into my eyes and talking in this very loud voice. ". . . So if I do have to wing it to the coast, love, I'll be on the horn daily. And tell me what kind of a surprise I can bring back for you. Earrings? Hoops? Small ones?"

I would have cracked up laughing if I hadn't felt so sorry for him. I mean, who talked like that? Half the time he didn't have the money to buy himself a second Coke in Corps, never mind earrings, hoops, small ones, from the coast.

As we passed The Pillars, I noticed Christine and Marlon Fredenberg standing together, and for Adam's sake I decided to play one last scene.

"Darling, I'm going to miss you fiercely," I said, hoping my voice didn't sound as phony to them as it sounded to me.

Marlon Fredenberg gave me this big wink. I had the distinct feeling it was his way of letting me know what a creep he thought I was, this laughable creep.

The bell was ringing.

Once we got inside, Adam let go of me.

I reached inside my coat pocket for his ring.

"Now she's playing up to Marlon Fredenberg," he said.

"We have to have a talk," I said.

"Marlon Fredenberg of all people!" he said.

I was turning the ring with my fingers. "There's nothing wrong with Marlon Fredenberg," I said. "Football captain, track star, basketball—"

Adam snapped, "Oh Brenda Belle, can it!"

It was a perfect moment for me to slap the ring into Adam's palm, which was exactly what I intended to do, when suddenly I noticed something about the ring that I'd never noticed before.

I managed to pursue the conversation. "Nothing Power isn't working," I said. "I cannot write another mash note to Ella Early. After three of them, she's the same old dark cloud. And look at us, Adam, look at—"

Just at that point, Miss Flexner, the principal's assistant, called out to Adam. "Mr. Blessing? Mr. Baird would like to see you in his office."

Adam walked away from me without saying anything.

I stood there examining the ring. Adam had said it was his father's school ring, but the last initial was not a B.

From the Journal of A.

It was still dark out when the telephone rang early that morning. My grandfather slept through it. He'd been drinking beer the night before; he'd called Late Night Larry to announce he was probably going into the restaurant business out on the coast. ("If you're ever out that way, stop into Chuck From Vermont's for a delicious meal." . . . "We certainly will," Late Night Larry had answered, "and we'll miss you, Chuck From Vermont!") My grandfather had gotten that new pipe dream from Billie Kay, who was busy sending him all sorts of information about franchise businesses.

It was my father calling, and I could tell by his voice he was feeling no pain.

"Someone here wants to meet you, A.J. Say hello."

150

I said, "Hello?"

"I've heard so much about you, A.J.," this female voice said.

"Who are you?" I asked as I groped for the light switch in the kitchen.

"Ha, ha, how silly of me, you don't even know me, do you, sweetie? Sweetie, this is Electra Lindgren."

"How do you do," I said. I sat down on the kitchen stool and stared at the sweet potato plant on the window sill. There were small green shoots all over its side.

"Is it snowing in Vermont?" Electric Socket asked me.

"Not right now," I said.

"Have you had a lot of snow this winter?"

My father's voice cut in. "Never mind all the small talk. A.J.?"

"Yes?"

"You may have to wing it out to the coast in two weeks for a wedding."

"Are you getting married?" I asked.

"What do you think I'm on the horn about at this hour?" I figured it was about three in the morning out there.

"Congratulations," I said.

"Your grandpa can come with you," my father said. "Billie Kay tells me he'd like to look around out here for a place to set up business."

"When did you see Billie Kay?" I said.

"We saw her yesterday. Jesus, she's aged!"

"I don't think she can help it," I said.

"What?"

"I said it happens to the best of us."

"What are you talking about, A.J.? Speak up!"

"I said none of us is getting any younger."

"A.J.," my father said, "never mind manifest knowledge at long-distance rates. Stick to the subject. We'll probably tie the knot around the fourteenth."

Electric Socket was back on the wire. "A.J.? We're going to have a very free ceremony. I'm writing the vows myself. You can wear jeans if you want to. We're going to be married in the desert."

"Fine," I said.

"A.J.," my father said, "I'll wire you some money." Then he began whispering. "Pick up a wedding gift from you to Electra. . . . Earrings? Can you pick out some simple gold earrings for pierced ears?"

"I guess so," I said.

"Hoops," he whispered. "Small ones. . . . Here's Electra again."

"A.J.? I just stepped away to get my notebook. Here's part of the ceremony I wrote myself. Are you listening?"

"Yes," I said.

"Okay. It goes, 'We are gathered here to marry two people who love each other.' That's the minister.

Then *I* go, 'I love you and want to live with you as long as you want to live with me.' Then your father goes, 'I love you and want to live with you as long as you want to live with me.' Then I go, 'I will care for you but never crowd you.' Then your father goes, 'I will care for you but—'"

My father's voice interrupted. "Never mind that now. A.J.?"

"Yes, sir?"

"You come out on the thirteenth. Bring your grandfather with you. Billie Kay will probably be calling him about it."

Electric Socket said, "Don't wear winter clothes because we'll be in the desert."

I said, "Dad?"

"What is it, A.J.?"

"Listen, should people know about this?"

"What do you mean?"

"I mean, should this be widely known?"

"You mean widely known in Storm, Vermont?" He laughed. He said, "You just get your tail out here and let me handle press relations."

"Yes, sir," I said.

"You're still incognito there, aren't you, or couldn't you stick to it?"

"I'm sticking to it," I said. "I'm not getting great grades. I flunked a history test last week."

"Here's Electra again, A.J.," my father said.

"A.J.? I want you to call me Electra. You don't have to call me 'Mother.' "

"Okay."

"Everyone's going to carry a small bunch of dandelions," she said. "I've always been partial to dandelions, and your father's promised to hunt down thousands and thousands of dandelions to pass around at the reception. They'll be my wedding bouquet, too. Imagine dandelions in the desert!"

Then my father said, "You'll go back the night of the fourteenth, A.J. Don't worry about anyone finding out who you are, you won't stay for the reception. You'll just wing it out for the private ceremony and then back to obscurity." He laughed.

"That suits me fine," I said.

"Maybe you'd better ask Billie Kay to pick out the earrings for you. I don't want you to buy something crappy."

"Is Billie Kay coming to the wedding?"

"Why should she? It's private. She can come to the reception. Everyone is invited to the reception," he said. "After all, a man only gets married once . . . or twice . . . or three times." He laughed so hard he had a short coughing fit. Then he said, "See you, A.J. Call me if you need anything."

I hung up when I heard the dial tone. For a while I sat staring at the sweet potato plant. I was remembering what Brenda Belle had said about beautiful things changing after a while . . . and I was wonder-

154

ing how long the glow would last between my father and Electric Socket.

I didn't want him to marry her, not because it probably wouldn't last, and not because I was particularly interested in my father's happiness. It was something else; it was the snide cracks in columns about the women he dated, and it was a cartoon a Washington paper had once printed. In the cartoon my father was at a conference table with some U.N. dignitaries. There was a balloon over his head, and inside it were all these naked females, young and big-busted: the types he dated. The balloon was supposed to represent what he was thinking while he was at the conference. He was wearing a tie pin with the initials D.O.M. (for Dirty Old Man), and the cartoon was captioned, "*In the Spring an Old Man's Fancy Lightly Turns from Thoughts of Peace.*"

I know my father laughed at things like that. "A.J.," he always said of the press, "the day they don't have it in for me, I don't have it anymore."

But things like that always bothered me. I had these long daydreams in which my mother was still alive . . . or if I felt that was asking too much, there was a stepmother, a woman with graying hair and a very poised and dignified facade . . . and we all lived together and were photographed coming out of church, or enjoying a family outing in some national park, feeding deer or roasting marshmallows over an open fire. Sometimes we ate dinner out (not in a nightclub) and other times my father carved a Thanksgiving turkey, and the table was filled with just ordinary relatives like Grandpa Blessing.

I knew my father had earned the right to behave any way he wanted, and I hadn't even earned the right to criticize him, but I could never understand his taste in women. I asked him once why he never liked the brainy types, and his answer was, "A.J., I have a very large library available for mental stimulation."

"He's just a man," Billie Kay used to say during her darkest moments with him. "I've got to get that through my head."

My grandfather was still asleep after I'd dressed and made myself a breakfast I couldn't finish. I put on my coat and began walking around Storm until it got light out.

What I was doing was what psychologists call "displacing"—concentrating hard on another problem to make the real problem less important. (I've seen several psychologists, mostly those employed by schools to help solve students' problems.) I was putting most of my attention on the forthcoming Valentine dance, muttering to myself over the fact I'd miss it because I'd be on the coast. At Storm High, the Valentine dance was traditionally a masquerade ball. Everyone came as a famous lover, and they all wore masks.

The mask idea really appealed to me, because Christine Cutler really appealed to me, and I'd been wearing a variety of invisible masks ever since New Year's Day. In one, I was Brenda Belle's boyfriend, playing the role to the hilt, hoping to make Christine jealous. In another, I was this dark and brooding fellow who passed her in the halls without looking at her, pretending to be too deep in thought to notice her. In still another, I was her secret admirer, watching her every move, standing near her in the shadows, exchanging these looks with her. That mask was the one she seemed to respond to the most. . . . I had envisioned myself stepping forward from the shadows at the Valentine dance.

I'd intended to go as the Shropshire Lad of Housman's poems, the one who'd been to Ludlow fair and left his necktie God knows where, and who'd heard a wise man say when he was one-and-twenty, "Give crowns and pounds and guineas, But not your heart away. . . ."

Housman was my favorite poet. I knew a lot of *A Shropshire Lad* from memory. My father said that Housman wasn't deep (my father preferred poets like Milton, Pope, Spender and Auden), but I believe he just didn't have enough heart for A. E. Housman. My father was the type who'd consider the Shropshire Lad a loser.

With all hopes of attending the dance crushed, I

felt this wave of fatigue coming over me as I walked around Storm. Like I said, I was displacing, thinking only of the dance and pushing from my mind the other things: my father's forthcoming marriage to Electric Socket, the old familiar down direction my school marks were heading in—the old familiar feeling of wanting to give up. When daylight came, I thought of going back to my grandfather's and sleeping through the day. Instead, I wound up at school and talked myself into staying awake.

I had a tendency toward narcolepsy. I never knew the word for it until my father told me about this famous senator who suffers from it. He falls asleep very suddenly, driving a car, eating dinner in a restaurant, during meetings, and particularly on the Senate floor. To combat it, he has to take pep-up pills constantly, so that he's often high and talkative and rowdy. There are rumors that he drinks, though he never touches a drop, and there are stories of his explosive temper and his restless inattentiveness during Senate proceedings. My father said when he's off the pills, he tries to stay awake by reciting isms: Communism, feudalism, paganism, masochism, et cetera.

I used to sleep away all my free time when I was attending private schools, and I often slept during class. Whenever the going got rough, I got sleepy. ("What is it you can't face?" one of the school psychologists had asked me once. "Why, being awake, I guess," I smirked. I got four demerits for that fast answer.) After my father told me about the Senator, I tried to keep myself awake reciting ations: sedation, nation, ration, conversation, et cetera.

For a while as I sat by the school that morning, I was going at a good clip: decimation, condemnation, deflation, cancellation, complication, aspiration, combination, gyration, on and on, and all the while I spent my time at that, it completely escaped my memory that I was supposed to have a poem which would depict "poignancy" ready for English.

Before I even got to English, there was my visit with the principal of Storm High.

"Sit down, Adam," he said, "I want to have a talk with you."

I sat across from his desk in a large leather chair. I sometimes think heads of schools all over the United States buy the large leather chairs across from their desks from the same place. They are all alike. The reason I have found myself sitting in one of them is never very different, either.

The principal's name was Mr. Baird. I'd met him only once before, on my first day in that school.

"What's the matter, sir?" I said.

"You tell me, Adam. Why are you failing three subjects? You're failing History, Math and Science."

"I seem to block on tests," I said. I remembered

another school psychologist telling me I was afraid to be tested, afraid I'd never measure up to my father.

"Adam," Mr. Baird said, "I know you haven't been with us very long, but would you say you're happy here in Storm?"

"I don't know, sir. I'm not unhappy, I don't think." It was going to happen again, I thought; it was beginning in the same old familiar way.

"Why have you been late getting to school?" he said. "I can understand oversleeping occasionally, but you have a total of nine lates with that excuse, all of them in three weeks' time."

"I don't have a good reason, I guess," I said. I remembered a story Billie Kay used to tell me about the movie star, Marilyn Monroe. Before she was famous, her name was Norma Jean Mortenson. She'd been this orphan child nobody'd ever wanted. After she became an important actress, she'd purposely take these long baths while everyone was waiting for her. She'd sit in the tub telling herself she was giving Norma Jean a treat: the whole world would have to wait for the little orphan kid nobody'd ever wanted.

I'd never purposely set out to make anyone wait for me, or been late on purpose, but I liked the story. I sat there distracting myself by thinking about it, because I had an idea what was coming. At one school they'd actually asked me to turn in my athletic sweater, because only graduates could own one.

I'd left this smelly purple-and-white sweater with holes under the arms on the headmaster's desk, as though I were surrendering an honor once bestowed on me and then rescinded.

"Adam," said Mr. Baird, "I wonder if it's working out, or if it isn't?"

"You don't think it's working out."

"Do you?"

"You want me to say it isn't, so you can say I should leave, or not return after Easter vacation. Isn't that right?"

He sighed. "Your father's asking a lot of you. You are who you are, Adam. You can't change that fact by changing your last name."

"My father didn't ask it of me. I asked it of me."

"You'll have to show some improvement, Adam."

"I will," I said. "Don't worry, I will."

"There's something else."

"What else?" I said.

"Dr. Cutler feels you're interested in Christine."

"In *Christine*?" I pretended to be dumbfounded at the idea.

"He says you've called her and you've been by the Cutlers'."

"Not lately," I said.

"And you haven't called lately without saying anything when she answered the phone?"

Twice. I'd done that exactly twice. I'd heard her

say "Hello" and then I'd clammed up. Maybe I'd never intended to say anything. I don't know. I'd dialed her number once after flunking the History test, and once one Saturday night after I had been over at Brenda Belle's and she was rattling on about Ty Hardin. . . . I knew Christine knew that it was me. I knew Christine was as aware of me as I was of her.

"Why would I do that?" I asked.

Mr. Baird shook his head. "I don't know why you would, either. Maybe Dr. Cutler is making something out of nothing. He has no love for Charlie and that feeling may extend to you."

"What exactly happened between them?" I asked.

Mr. Baird said, "Whatever happened between them is something probably only they know. Feuds are like that. There are rumors and versions and the real truth is obscured. I don't know what happened between them. Ask your grandfather what happened between them."

"I have," I said. "He said Dr. Cutler stole his business from him." My grandfather had never said that outright; Marlon Fredenberg had said that. I was testing to see what I could find out.

Mr. Baird just shrugged. "Well then." He leaned back in his chair. "Adam, the point is I can't tell Dr. Cutler anything about your background when he asks me. I have to pretend I don't know that much about you. . . . You can see why Dr. Cutler doesn't encourage your interest in Christine."

"Why does he have to know who my father is?" I said.

"He's got a right to know something about you."

"I see," I said.

"*Do* you?"

"Yes," I said, "I see."

"That's what I meant when I said this situation is asking a lot of you. It may be the reason you're having trouble."

"Either way," I said, "I'd probably be having trouble."

"What?" he said.

"I said I won't be any more trouble."

"I hope not," he said.

I was late getting to English. I saw Christine sitting in the front row. She gave me this look, the same kind of look I'd been giving her and she'd been giving me for weeks now. It was one of those long looks that cries out for words which you could probably never say if you knew the right words, anyway. You certainly couldn't say them in front of someone's locker, or passing someone in the hall, or sitting in Corps Drugs over Cokes. She knew about the look and so did I, but every time we were close enough to talk, we didn't look at each other and we said stupid things, like the day she said, "Stop staring at me, you're always staring at me," and I said, "You must be staring back to know I'm always staring at you."

Another time I'd said, "Tell your father Billie Kay Case doesn't think I'm an unknown quantity," and she'd said, "A lot of people don't believe that was really Billie Kay Case, Adam."

We didn't have conversations, just fragments of conversations. What we had were these long looks between us.

As I was walking back to my seat, Miss Netzer said, "Don't bother to sit down yet, Adam. Since you're the last to arrive, you can be the first to recite."

"Recite?" I said.

"The poem you chose to depict poignancy," she said. "Step up in front of the class, Adam."

I had to do some fast thinking, since I had nothing prepared. I remembered the poem from *A Shropshire Lad* which I'd blocked on during that test at Choate. I knew it by heart, and I supposed it expressed poignancy as well as any other.

I put down my books on my desk and went to the front of the room.

"It's a poem by A. E. Housman. It's called 'The New Mistress.'"

"Proceed," she said.

I didn't want to look in Christine's direction. I saw Brenda Belle sitting in the second row, and I concentrated on her.

164

Then I began:

Oh, sick I am to see you, will you never let me be?
You may be good for something but you are not
*   good for me.*
Oh, go where you are wanted, for you are not wanted
*   here.*
And that was all . . .

And that *was* all; that was exactly where I had
blocked during the test at Choate, and exactly the
point where I began to laugh as I stood before Miss
Netzer's class.

I just laughed, first in small spurts with a few
words in between and then in great gales until I was
shaking and holding myself, laughing so hard it was
like crying.

I think what triggered it was the expression on
Brenda Belle's face, a slow, crumbling look of sad-
ness and disbelief, and I suddenly realized she
thought I was giving her a message. But I was not
really laughing because she had misunderstood and
I had hurt her: I was laughing at the messes we get
ourselves into, at the sheer craziness that exists, at
the victims we become, all of us.

"Adam? ADAM!" I heard Miss Netzer trying to
get my attention. I heard her rap the desk with her
ruler. But I couldn't stop.

"Sit down!" I heard. "Adam, sit down!"

But I was loose and convulsed, and by that time

very far away from that English class and everyone in it. My mind was racing compulsively, flashing pictures at me: pictures of myself packing my bags while the other boys went on to their classes, arriving at airports where my father waited with a new game plan etched in his eyes, a new school catalog for me to look through. . . . I saw our home in Virginia, where the housekeeper would serve me nightly as I sat by myself in the large dining room at the long oak table; I saw my father getting out of a helicopter on the White House lawn while I watched him on the boob tube miles away; I saw that Polaroid picture of my mother and my father and me with our faces missing; and I saw a wedding in the desert filled with dandelions while Electric Socket "went" "I will care for you but not crowd you," and my father "went" "I will care for you but not crowd you—"

"Leave the room immediately, Adam!" Miss Netzer had me by my arm.

Then I was out in the hall.

"Adam Blessing, is anything wrong?"

I turned around to see who it was, and beheld a tender, smiling face, a bright clean flower-splotched dress in blue and yellow, a vision: It was Ella Early, her gray hair freed from the bun and newly curled; Ella Early, soft-toned and minus chalk dust . . . Ella Late Who Has No Fate, transformed and shining with Nothing Power.

Notes for a Novel by B.B.B.

"Better a quiet death," my mother is fond of saying, "than a public humiliation."

I experienced both after Adam recited that poem in English while looking straight at me. In fact, I died quietly several times, and the most painful of all my deaths was when Christine Cutler turned around in her seat and smirked at me.

After that, I carried a quotation in my wallet which I had copied from an essay by William Hazlitt: "Love turns, with a little indulgence, to indifference or disgust; hatred alone is immortal." Under the quotation, I wrote: *My attitude re: C.C.*

My mother says always have on nice underwear in case you are in an accident; if I was in an accident, I wanted it on record that I hated Christine Cutler.

It was five days before I could bring myself to

speak to Adam. He finally cornered me one afternoon when I was on my way to gym.

"You have to speak to me," he said. "I'm in enough trouble without you giving me the Silent Treatment."

"Don't tell me your troubles!" I said. "I am a laughingstock."

"I'm sorry," he said. "It wasn't intentional; it had nothing to do with you."

"Tell that to Ty Hardin," I said. "Do you know what he calls me? He calls me Sick I Am To See You."

"Who cares about Ty Hardin?" said Adam angrily.

"I do," I said. "We weren't sitting on our hands discussing religion on New Year's Eve."

"Oh for Pete's sake!" Adam said. "He's got a thing for Diane Wattley, Brenda Belle!"

It was news to me.

I said, "I have to run, old buddy. I have a date with a hockey stick."

"Wait a minute!" Adam said.

"Toodle-oo," I called out as I rushed past him.

It was my Aunt Faith who convinced me that I should go to Adam, return the ring after all, and tell him we should just be friends.

I had told both my Aunt Faith and my mother about the initials on the ring. I had done it the night of the day of my humiliation in English, when I was still furious with Adam. When I showed them the ring, I said, "I think he's an impostor! I happen to know he was kicked out of private school, too, and that's why he's here in Storm."

At first they asked me a lot of questions about Adam and Christine Cutler and all that had happened. Then they seemed to lose interest in the subject, and my mother got that tight little expression around her mouth that meant she no longer wanted to discuss something.

Shortly after my conversation with Adam, one afternoon when I was home from school early (because my mustache was growing in again very faintly, and I had work to do in the privacy of my bathroom with a jar of peroxide), my aunt appeared in my room.

"You should return the ring, Brenda Belle," she said. "After all, you yourself admitted that Nothing Power hasn't worked."

"It's worked for Ella Early," I said. "She's transformed."

"Never mind Ella Early, dear. Don't you think you should talk with Adam, and give him back his ring?"

"And ask him what the initials mean, too," I said.

"I wouldn't pry, dear."

"I would," I said.

"But why, Brenda Belle?"

"Because I feel like it," I said. "Ty Hardin says what feels right is right."

I wondered why my mother and my aunt weren't more excited about my discovery that the last initial was not a B. They were both capable of getting excited over a lot less than that. My mother often returned from the hairdresser reeling with the news that some afternoon soap-opera star was having a marital tiff, and my Aunt Faith often did her needlework in my mother's car, parked down on Main Street early Saturday evenings, so she could see who was on his way to the movies with whom.

It was snowing out as I walked down the hill to Dr. Blessing's. I hoped it would continue for a week without stopping, set some kind of unheard-of disaster record and prevent anyone from leaving his house for days on end. . . . The Valentine dance was only five days away, and I did not have a date.

Ty Hardin's interest in Diane Wattley was a blow. Anyone but Diane Wattley, who had bowlegs and pronounced all her r's like w's. If I couldn't compete with a Diane Wattley, I was the next thing to a basket case. When Christine Cutler (hatred alone is immortal!) was my competition, I had an excuse, but now what I had was plain old me back on my hands again, complete with dreams of nooses, razor blades and Greyhound buses to New York City. . . . Even Ella Early had more hope.

Dr. Blessing answered the door wearing his new

sport coat, plus a scarf knotted around his neck like an ascot.

"Come on in, Brenda Belle," he said. "I'm busy packing. Close the door after you."

I said, "You must be excited about going to the coast."

"I don't get excited at my age," he said, racing around carrying shirts and socks from a bureau in the living room to a suitcase on the couch.

"Are you leaving so early? I thought Adam said he was leaving the thirteenth?"

"The thirteenth isn't far away," he said.

"It's five days away."

"I have to be all packed," he said.

"Is Adam packing this early?"

"Adam isn't packing. Adam isn't going."

"Why isn't Adam going?"

"Adam's on probation, Brenda Belle. Where have you been?"

I said, "I didn't know."

"He can't go anywhere. Hand me my spritzer."

"Your what?"

"My spritzer, my spritzer. Over there."

I handed him the glass he pointed to.

"What's a spritzer?"

"It's wine with soda," he said. "Billie Kay Case drinks them. The soda dilutes the wine so you don't get too much wine."

He drank what was in the glass in one gulp.

"You mean you're going but Adam isn't?" I said. "I thought Adam was going because of something to do with his father."

"He can't go, but I'm going, anyway . . . on business."

He went into the kitchen and made himself another spritzer. I saw the sweet potato plant on the window. The water was brown.

I said, "You have to change the water or this plant will die."

"*I* don't have to change it," he said. "I have to pack."

I took off my coat and changed the water in the plant. I cut off the brown leaves and turned the new sprouts toward the light.

Dr. Blessing was rushing around singing, "Hel-lo from Hol-ly-wood" and making more spritzers as he packed. Each new drink was darker in color. He was ordering me to hand him this and fetch him that, and I finally said, "When exactly do you expect Adam?"

"He'll be along. Fold that sweater for me."

"Listen, I am not the maid," I said.

He wasn't paying any attention to what I said, so I finally sat down and wrote Adam a note.

Dear Adam, I'm returning your ring because Nothing Power is a flop, but I want to be friends.

*Friends should tell things to each other, like why is
your father's last initial not a B? Does "probation"
mean you can't go to the dance, or do you want to
escort a friend to it? You owe me that. BBB.*

While I was putting the ring and the note on top
of Adam's Latin notebook, the phone rang.

"I'll be leaving now," I said. "There's something
there for Adam."

As I went out the door, Dr. Blessing was telling
someone who had telephoned that he did not care
what the dog's temperature was, that he had more
important things to worry about than an animal's
temperature.

When I got back to my house, I could see my
mother and my aunt sitting in the living room. I got
this idea to sneak in the back door, go down on all
fours, crawl toward the living room, and then spring
out at them like the girl in *Teen-age Vampire*.

I made it as far as the dining room, when I caught
the drift of their conversation and stopped in my
tracks.

"Annabell Blessing never married a man that
famous," my mother was saying. "I can't remember
his name, but he was a nobody, a lawyer of some
kind from New York."

"Way back then he was," said my aunt. "He
could have *become* famous."

"Not that famous, Faith!"

"The initials are the same, Millie, and that would also explain Billie Kay Case's arrival at Christmas. She was his second wife, and she must have been the boy's stepmother!"

"I, for one, don't believe it," said my mother. "Not that boy living down there with Charlie, tying those beer cans to the Christmas tree!"

"After all, Millie, a former neighbor doesn't travel to Vermont for Christmas, but a stepmother would!"

"I don't want Brenda Belle to know anything about this conversation," said my mother. "I don't want to dig up old bones. I doubt the Cutler child knows anything about her father and Annabell Blessing."

My Aunt Faith said, "Oh, very few know that. Doc Hendricks saw to that for Charlie's sake, when he was called in as coroner. Doc even testified that Annabell was alone in the car, testified to an untruth."

"Told a lie that Annabell was alone in the car! Perjured himself!" said my mother. "Ted Cutler walked away from that accident without a scratch to his body or his reputation!"

"What good would it have done, Millie, if Doc *had* let the truth be known? It would only have done harm to everyone!"

My mother said, "Annabell Blessing and Ted Cutler should have thought of that when they tried to run off like that! Both of them married to other people, both with small children. Disgusting!"

"And water over the dam," said my aunt.

"If that boy *is* Annabell's son, I wonder if *he* knows his mother was killed trying to run off with Ted."

"I'm sure he doesn't," said my aunt.

"For the son of someone that famous," said my mother, "he's certainly unimpressive, living down there with Charlie."

I stood up at the pause in that conversation, and tiptoed back through the kitchen, and out the door . . . the same way I'd come in, except nothing was really going to be the same again. I knew that much.

From the Journal of A.

I remember something my father once told me about the word "crisis," when it's written in Chinese. It's composed of two characters: One represents danger and the other represents opportunity.

That was certainly true of my probation crisis.

On the one hand Dr. Baird summoned me to his office after my scene in English, and told me that if I was absent from a class, or late for a class, if I misbehaved in a class, or flunked another test—*fini.* "You are now on probation, Adam," he said, "and you are in danger of being expelled."

On the other hand, as I walked away from his office, two people were waiting for me at the end of the hall. One was Marlon Fredenberg. The other was Christine.

"Adam," she said, "Marlon's my good friend. We can talk in front of Marlon. Is everything okay? What did Mr. Baird say?"

"For one thing, I'm supposed to stay away from you," I said. "Your father's orders."

"I know about that," she said. "That's why Marlon's with me. We can just walk along and talk, like I'm really with Marlon."

"And I'm on probation," I said. Then I told her the rest while the three of us walked out to the parking lot where Marlon's old Chevy was. I was so shook up, it barely registered with me that Christine wasn't playing games with me any longer, that she was actually concerned, that we were actually having a serious conversation. Marlon didn't say anything. He just walked along with us, like he was our guard, blocking us from any interference, as he protected teammates during football games on Saturday afternoons.

We drove around Storm for about an hour, talking all the time.

"What's the *matter* with your father?" I asked Christine. "Why is he so dead set against me?"

"I can't really figure it out," she said. "Part of it's because he really resents your grandfather telling everyone he stole the business from him."

"My grandfather never told me that," I said.

"He told other people that," she said, "and it

really isn't fair. After your Aunt Annabell's accident, my father ran the Storm Animal Shelter single-handed. Charlie was drinking. My father only drew a small salary—he gave the rest to Charlie, for years. He finally bought Charlie out because Charlie wasn't doing any of the work."

"Don't call him Charlie," I said. "That hasn't got anything to do with me, even if it is true."

"I know that," Christine said, "but he doesn't know anything about you. Then he got this strange card, about remembering someone he left behind. He has the idea you sent it."

"Why?" I said.

She said, "I don't know. Maybe he thinks the someone refers to Charlie. Maybe he thinks you're trying to tell him he left Charlie behind. He won't talk about it."

Marlon said, "I have to have the car back by four thirty. My mother's going to Burlington."

"We have an idea, Adam," Christine said. "See what you think about it."

This is where the "opportunity" came into the picture.

Christine said we could see each other with Marlon "fronting" for us. Marlon would call for her and take her home, but her date would really be with me.

We began to make plans, and before long we were all three laughing and anticipating the scheme like it was a fabulous adventure we were about to embark on. We made a vow to keep it a secret from everyone else; as far as everyone else was concerned, Christine would be going with Marlon. The only time we'd make an exception would be when Marlon wanted to date someone: She'd have to be let in on the scheme, because she'd have to pose as my date.

"Let's make our first date the Valentine dance," Christine said.

Marlon said, "We can't. The team plays Stowe that Saturday. I won't be back in Storm until around eleven that night."

Basketball was not the big thing football was at Storm High, but we had a team, of sorts, and Marlon was a basketball star, too.

Christine looked disappointed for a while, and then her eyes brightened.

"It doesn't matter," she said. "It's a costume ball. Adam can wear a disguise and pretend he's you, Marlon."

"What if your father recognizes my voice when I pick you up?" I said.

"There has to be a way around that," Christine said. "Think of a disguise that makes it impossible for you to talk."

"A dummy of some kind," said Marlon.

"Something or someone that doesn't speak," Christine said.

"Someone without a head," I said.

"Mary, Queen of Scots," said Marlon.

I said, "I'm *not* going in drag."

"*I* know!" Christine said. "Sir Walter Raleigh! *He* was beheaded! You can wear a costume that completely covers your face, carry this head, and have this muddy cloak with you that Raleigh put down for Queen Elizabeth!"

We settled on Sir Walter.

I felt Christine's hand sneak into mine and we held hands hard while Marlon drove me to my grandfather's.

The first thing I did when I got inside was place a long distance call to my father. I waited for him to explode when I announced that I was on probation, but after I was finished telling him about it, he said, "Well, maybe it's a godsend."

"What?" I said.

"I may have to make a trip, anyway," he said.

"What about the wedding?"

"We had a lot to drink last night, A.J."

"Oh," I said. "Is there going to be a wedding?"

"It isn't firm," he said.

Then he said, "How did you manage to get into difficulty so fast, A.J.? You set a record this time."

"I'm going to be all right from now on," I said. "Don't worry about me."

He said, "A.J.? I may have to make a trip. Some

mail addressed to me may come care of you at that address. Just hang on to it. I'll be in touch."

I should have perceived the fact that that was a strange arrangement, but that afternoon very little seemed to register but the fact that Christine had come my way, and who my father was had nothing to do with it.

My grandfather went ahead with his plan to visit Billie Kay. He changed in the next few days, and I changed, too. We began to get in each other's way and talk at each other instead of with each other. I didn't discuss Christine with him, but one night when he was loading himself up on these spritzers Billie Kay had taught him to drink, I managed to question him about his feud with Christine's father.

"Did he or didn't he steal your business?" I said.

"He was responsible," he answered.

"Didn't he run your business, though, and pay you most of the profit?"

"Do you know how the Puritans used to eat dinner?" he said.

"Stick to the subject," I said.

"They ate at a trestle table," he said. "The younger children stood near the foot and didn't speak, and the master of the house sat at the head. Just pretend there's a trestle table between us."

"Thank you, Chuck From Vermont," I said.

He had taken to wearing a scarf knotted around his neck, and he was rarely out of that sport coat he'd originally said was too good for him.

He was in his world and I was in mine. His began to irritate me as it never had since I'd come to live with him. I became aware of how noisy he was as I increased my studying, determined to bring up my grades. If the television wasn't on, the radio was. He was packing and unpacking incessantly, hanging up on people who called for advice about their ill animals and determinedly killing wine bottles at night.

I set my sights on the time he would be out on the coast. I lived for that time. I had long, involved daydreams about Christine and myself alone together in the house. In a way, Marlon's presence added to the excitement when we went for drives after school, but I wanted to be alone with Christine.

One afternoon when I returned from another of our excursions in Marlon's old Chevy, Brenda Belle's note and my ring were waiting for me.

I called her up.

"I'm all for being friends," I said. "I can explain about the ring."

"You don't have to," she said.

"My father's ring got mixed up with another student's ring and—"

"I don't care!" she cut me off sharply. "You don't have to explain anything."

"You said you wanted me to explain," I said.

"I don't want you to explain anything," she said. "Friends don't have to explain anything."

"You just finished writing me a note saying friends had to tell each other things."

"Friends don't," she said.

"About the dance," I said.

"You don't have to take me."

"I probably won't go."

"Because you're on probation?"

"Yes," I lied.

"I'm sorry you're in trouble," she said. "I mean that. I'm really sorry."

"Why the change?" I said.

"Why not the change? We're due for a change. I'm sorry you're in trouble and if I can ever do anything to help you out, I'll do it."

"Why are you talking so fast?" I said.

"I feel like talking fast."

"You sound nervous."

"I'm not nervous."

"Then we're friends?"

"To the death," she said.

"What are we going to do about Ella Early?" I asked.

"What *should* we do about her?"

"Are we just going to stop writing her mash notes now, just click off?"

"*We* didn't write her mash notes. *I* wrote her mash notes."

"Are you just going to click off?"

"You said yourself life isn't fair, even or equal."

As time flew by I began to think I was wrong about life. I began to believe life, like the Lord, giveth and taketh, and suddenly I was on the giveth side. . . . My father was not going to marry Electric Socket; Christine was mine; there was an empty house all to myself in my near future; Brenda Belle was my friend. . . . I had even passed a surprise history quiz with a B–.

My grandfather left for California on the morning of the thirteenth. After school that afternoon, I rushed home to clean the house from top to bottom. I must have made twelve trips from the kitchen to the workshed, carrying out empty gallon bottles of Almadén wine. I moved the furniture around, washed windows, changed sheets, polished woodwork and scrubbed the bathroom.

Then after I made myself dinner, I set to work on my Sir Walter costume. Around eight o'clock, Christine called me. Her folks were at the movies. She was working on her costume, too; she was going as Queen Elizabeth.

We had one of these long conversations where

184

what you said wasn't important ("What are you thinking?" . . . "Things." . . . "*What* things?" . . . "Things about you." . . . "Like what?" et cetera) but you felt like you were reciting Elizabeth Barrett Browning's love sonnets to each other, and you could hear each other breathing, and your palms were wet.

At one point I said, "I wish you'd come here."

"I wish I could."

"Can't you?"

"I don't want to spoil anything for tomorrow night."

"Can't you sneak over for a while?"

"I'm afraid to risk it."

"I really wish you were here."

"Me too."

"Me too."

Like that.

After I hung up, I turned on the radio and listened to the words of hit songs, turning the dial when the song on one station didn't seem to apply to Christine and me, switching around finding the right songs. I stayed there on the couch that way for about an hour, higher than a kite on Coke and Christine and the second character in the Chinese word for "crisis."

Then the knock came on the door.

My feet didn't feel as though they were touching the floor as I went to answer it. In those seconds

185

life was fair, even, equal and fantastic, and I was grinning; I was ripping apart inside with this wild feeling, brimming over.

I flung open the door and said, "You came!"

"I had to!" she said.

I just looked at her then for several slow beats.

"I couldn't let your father go through this alone," Electric Socket said; "but shouldn't you be in bed, honey?"

She was carrying a suitcase.

Notes for a Novel by B.B.B.

"Adam," I said, "this is Brenda Belle."

"I know who it is," he said.

Bear in mind that I was seeing him in an entirely new light, and that, in a way, it was like calling up a stranger. I had made up my mind to keep my big mouth shut concerning all that I had learned about him.

"Since neither of us is going to the dance tonight," I said, "why don't we get together?"

"What time is it?" he said.

"What do you mean what time is it?"

"What *time* is it?"

"It is twelve o'clock noon."

"It is?"

"What's the matter with you?" I asked.

"I've been up all night."

"Why?"

"I've been handling something, Brenda Belle."

"Handling what?"

"Something came up."

"What's going on?"

"Call me back."

"When?"

"*I'll* call *you*," he said.

From the Journal of A.

"*I'll* call *you*," I told Brenda Belle.

"I've heard that one before," she said.

I said, "I will," and I hung up just as Electric Socket came out of the bathroom. She was wearing the red silk gown with the mink collar and cuffs which she'd changed into the night before. For a while after she'd first arrived, I'd just sat across from her in the living room, listening to her. My father had postponed the wedding with the excuse that I was very sick and that he had to be with me. He had told her not to telephone, but that she could write to this address. She'd decided to just hop a jet and join him.

"He's always been such a big baby, A.J.," she'd

told me. "Do you know what he always said when he hugged me tight?"

"No," I'd answered, not wanting to hear.

" 'Never leave me, never leave me, never leave me no matter what.' He'd say that over and over and over."

"I'm sorry," I'd said, because I'd been unable to think of anything else to say.

"Who was that on the telephone just then, A.J.?" she said.

"A friend," I said.

"It wasn't him, was it?"

"No, honestly, Electra. Why don't you try to sleep now? You haven't had any sleep."

"I'll sleep," she said. "I'll sleep," but she sat down in my grandfather's leather chair and picked up the silver flask filled with bourbon, which she'd been nursing along through most of the night. Her eyelids were beginning to droop, and her mascara was running. "Read me the Bible," she said in this thick-tongued voice.

"Look, Electra," I said, "I'm not good at reading the Bible."

She pulled the head I'd made of Sir Walter Raleigh into her lap and began stroking the black hair I'd fashioned from darning thread.

"The Bible is the only thing that calms me," she said.

I was beginning to worry about what I was going

to do with her when it came time for me to get ready
for the dance.

"I don't even know if my grandfather has a Bible."

"Corinthians," she mumbled.

I said, "If it'll help you sleep, I'll try to find a
Bible."

"I want to die," she said.

"I'll *find* a Bible."

I ran into my grandfather's bedroom. She'd un-
packed on the bed and her stuff was all over the
place: a blonde wig, undies, half a dozen fashion
magazines. I looked everywhere for a Bible, but I
couldn't find one. From the other room, I could hear
her babbling. " 'When I was a child, I spake as a
child. . . .' "

I stumbled over one of her shoes and cursed everything. Coffee, I thought, strong coffee to sober her
up, and as I raced into the kitchen, I saw the flaw in
that idea: Coffee would only keep her awake. I stood
there trying desperately to think of some plan of
action, when my eyes rested on the telephone book in
a corner of the old wooden counter. Under the telephone book was a thick volume with red-gold pages
and a purple ribbon hanging from it. I had never
noticed it before, but it was very definitely a Bible.

While I was lifting it up, a piece of paper fell out
of it, faded blue and old, with handwriting across it.
I reached down and picked it up, and saw the sig-
nature. "Annabell."

I called in to Electric Socket, "Just a second! I see a Bible!"

"First Corinthians, Chapter Thirteen!" she shouted back.

I held the piece of paper in my hands and read my mother's writing.

Dearest Daddy,

I know my phone call tonight came as a shock, but please don't worry about me anymore. You don't have to worry about me anymore, Daddy. He's a really decent man, kind and intelligent—he's very intelligent, with more books in his library than there are in the Storm library, and he's actually read them all, too. Daddy, he loves me so very much, and I am really going to learn to love him back. As I told you, he's a lawyer, but he doesn't want to practice law all his life. He is ambitious and hard-working. Don't worry about me, Daddy. More than anything else now, I want to get pregnant and have a baby and grow to love my husband. I'm not too homesick but it's still a big city. I think becoming a mother will grow me up, too, and my husband is patient and says he has enough love in his heart for the two of us. I think this is the answer. I have the answer now, Daddy, so take care of yourself and don't worry.

Love,
Annabell.

"Thy kingdom come!" Electric Socket said from the other room.

"I'm coming, Electric," I said, folding the letter and putting it in my trouser pocket.

I lugged the Bible into the living room where she was sitting, with her head dangling as though it hung by a thread.

"Corinthians?" I said, flipping through the Bible as I sat down on the hassock next to her chair.

"Good-bye, A.J.," she said.

"Are you going to sleep?" I said. "Don't you want to go into the bedroom?"

"I'm here," she said. "Good-bye."

"Sweet dreams," I said, as she closed her eyes and sighed.

I picked up the overflowing ashtray and emptied it in the kitchen. I kept thinking about my mother's letter, and the date at the top, and I did some fast arithmetic. My mother was just about four years older than me when she wrote that to my grandfather. I had such a completely different picture of her after I read that letter. It wasn't only the punch of shock at the fact she'd never loved my father, and he'd known that when he married her; it was the vulnerability she expressed, the wistful "don't worry's" and the "I think this is the answer," followed by "I have the answer," as though she was trying so hard to talk herself into something.

I was close to tears . . . maybe because I hadn't slept all night. I had the feeling I was just going to break down and bawl my guts out. I went into the bathroom to stick my head under a faucet of cold water.

It was then that I found the empty bottle marked Nembutal.

Notes for a Novel by B.B.B.

"You took your sweet time calling back," I said. "It's seven thirty. I'm all alone on a Saturday night, with only the boob tube for—"

"Brenda Belle," he said, "I don't have time to talk. This is an emergency. I'm at the hospital with a friend of my father's. She tried to commit suicide."

"*Who* tried to commit suicide?"

"I can't go into it now," he said. "Brenda Belle, you said a few days ago that you'd do anything you could for me."

"That's true," I said.

"I'm asking you to do something for me now. Something very, very important, Brenda Belle."

"Okay," I said.

"Do you promise to do it?"

"I said *okay*!"

"Promise," he said.

"I *promise*, Adam!"

Never, never, never promise before you know what you are promising.

You may find yourself one fine evening dressed as a man, carrying the head of Sir Walter Raleigh, en route to a Valentine dance with Queen (hatred is immortal!) Elizabeth.

"Don't forget to spread your cloak at my feet so I can walk across it when we get inside," Christine Cutler said as we approached the gym.

"$%¢&*@#!" I answered.

"Brenda Belle, I can't hear a thing you're saying with that sweater over your face, so don't try to talk."

Her father had dropped us off in the parking lot.

"I want her home by one o'clock, Marlon," he'd said to me. "Not one thirty, not one fifteen, not one ten. One o'clock on the dot!"

I'd nodded my head up and down in assent and plowed through the snow a little ahead of Christine. She'd reached out and yanked me back. She was still hanging on to me.

"You're being a real good sport about this, Brenda Belle," she said. "I hope Adam's all right. I hope that friend of his father's doesn't die and spoil things so he can't get here. He said he'd get here, though, so she must be coming out of it. She's probably having her stomach pumped. I remember when old Mrs. Yarrow gave her basset hound a lot of tranquilizers to quiet him down, and my father had to pump out his stomach—*that* was a night to beat all nights! . . . Brenda Belle, don't tread on my train, please."

"STOP THE CHATTER! THE CHATTER MAKES ME NERVOUS!" I shouted.

"Don't shout," she said. "You can be heard."

"IT'S ABOUT TIME!" I said.

"Shhhh, Brenda Belle, people will know you're a girl."

We went inside and Queen Elizabeth hied herself off to the Girls', while I stood there carrying my head and praying to God my bladder would hold out through the evening. Adam had promised that he'd arrive with a woman's coat and a blonde wig for me to change into, and that by the time he got there, Marlon Fredenberg would have shown up to be my date. Adam would then take over as Sir Walter Raleigh, and we'd all double.

While I waited for Christine, I tore at one of the air holes in the sweater, making it wider so I could breathe and talk.

"For God's sake, don't bite your nails," Christine said as she approached from behind. "Sir Walter Raleigh didn't bite his nails."

"How am I supposed to be introduced?" I said. "It's one thing for your father to think I'm Marlon

197

Fredenberg, but all the kids know Marlon's in Stowe with the basketball team."

"You're the Mystery Man," she said. "If you have to speak, speak in a very low voice."

"I already have a very low voice," I said, "or haven't you noticed?"

The band was playing a slow number as we entered the gym. The lights were very low, and everyone was dancing except the boys who came stag and the girls on Wallflower Row whose dates were ignoring them.

Christine kept punching my side with her elbow, signaling for me to spread my cloak at her feet. When I finally did it, she said, "Thank you, Sir Walter," in this loud voice, and walked across it with this snotty expression on her face.

Then she said, "Well? Pick it up."

"You pick it up," I said.

"Queen Elizabeth didn't pick it up," she said. "Use your head."

"I don't have a head," I said, beginning to enjoy myself.

"Pick up the cloak!" she commanded.

"Don't make a scene," I said.

"I thought you were a good sport."

"I have my limits," I said.

She bent down and picked up the cloak with two fingers. "Yiiiik! It's dirty."

"That's why *I* didn't pick it up," I said.

"What'll I do with it?"

"Give it to me," I said.

She handed it to me, and I hung it across her shoulders. "So you won't feel the draft," I said.

"#%&¢$*#@, Brenda Belle!" She slapped the cloak back at me.

"You can be heard," I reminded her. "Lower your voice or everyone will know you date girls."

"You got my gown filthy!" she muttered under her breath.

"Let's dance," I said, shaking out the cloak and fastening it across my shoulders.

She began to sneeze from the dust.

I grabbed hold of her and began pushing her around the floor. "Isn't this fun?" I said. "You're a good sport, Christine."

"Get off my toes," she said.

I said, "You dance divinely."

"You don't," she said.

"Beggars can't be choosers."

"Keep that head away from my bare back," she said.

"We really need some ketchup for that head," I said. "Heads bleed when they're cut off."

"Don't talk," she said. "Do you *have* to talk?"

"What kind of a date would I be if I didn't talk?"

"Then don't talk about blood, please."

"That head should not only have blood dripping off it, there should be icky pieces of flesh and torn purple tendons extending from it."

"Will you shut up?"

"And pus probably, too; it'd be infected by this time," I said; "or it'd have maggots starting to collect on it."

"*Why* are you doing this?" she said.

"I wouldn't do it to everyone," I told her. "Only a select few, like the select few you had over on Christmas Eve."

"So that's it! Can't you forgive and forget?"

"I've forgiven," I said, "but I haven't forgotten. . . . Excuse me, was that your big toe?"

Ty Hardin was making his way across the dance floor, heading in our direction. He was dressed like a prince, and in case no one got the point, he had a name tag across his chest with ROMEO printed on it in large letters.

Christine said, "Don't let him cut in. I'm not speaking to him."

"I thought he was going with Diane Wattley."

"He is. He brought her here. I saw her in the girls' room."

"He's not with her now," I said.

"Well, he's not going to be with me, not for one second."

Ty tapped me on the shoulder a minute later.

"This is my dance," he said to me.

"Thanks," I said making my voice as low as possible. "I was bored stiff!" Then I walked away, leaving Christine with him.

I saw Marilyn Pepper standing over in Wallflower Row, dressed as a flapper from the twenties. Her parents always forced her brother to bring her to dances, and her brother always spent a lot of time out in the parking lot smoking.

I bowed very low as I stood in front of her. She had done a fairly good job of hiding her pimples with pancake makeup.

"Who are you?" she said.

I gave a shrug and bowed low again.

As we danced, she said, "Do I know you?"

Another shrug, but I pulled her closer. "I am your secret friend."

"Did you send me that card?"

I nodded.

"Milton Merrensky, is that you?"

I shrugged. Milton Merrensky was the shyest boy in Storm. I had never even seen him at a dance. He was rumored to have an IQ of 160, and you could find him any Saturday morning down in Hogg's Swamp, doing birdcalls, with binoculars around his neck.

Marilyn Pepper was smiling. "How did you make that head, Milton?" She had a nice smile. I didn't say anything, and we just danced and she smiled, and when the band played a fast number she said, "I can't dance fast ones." I led her back to Wallflower Row. Before I walked away, I said, "Don't forget me," in the same low voice.

I looked out at the dancers and saw Christine with Ty. They were not dancing. She was pointing her finger at him and there was this mean expression on her face, and he was backing away. Then she was standing in the center of the dance floor alone, looking all around. I knew she was looking for me. I walked in the opposite direction, past the chaperones.

Ella Late Who Has No Fate was standing at the end of the line. She was wearing the same new blue-and-yellow dress she'd been wearing nonstop for about two and a half weeks now. I stopped in front of her and bowed low.

"Oh, no," she said. "I don't dance. . . . Is it you, Adam?"

I shrugged.

She said, "Really, I don't dance. Thank you, anyway. *Is* it you, Adam?"

I whispered, "Did you get my notes?"

Her face became bright red, but she was pleased, as well as slightly embarrassed—I could tell that from her expression. She said, "Pay attention to your lessons, not me."

"You're my inspiration," I whispered.

"Then study!" she whispered back.

"I will!" I blew her a kiss and hurried on.

Out of the corner of my eye, I saw Christine heading for Wallflower Row.

I had a fine time. I danced with Sue Ellen Chayka, whose nose resembles a baboon's (she was there with Danton Trice, who weighed in at 214 and sat out most fast numbers), and after Christine got off Wallflower Row (it didn't take the boys in the stag line long to spot her there), I danced with Marilyn Pepper again, and got her a glass of punch before sailing off mysteriously.

After about an hour, I went out to the parking lot where some boys were smoking. I needed some fresh air after being cooped up inside that sweater. Marilyn's brother, Peter Pepper, was standing there drinking some Strawberry Ripple Wine he had secreted in a brown paper bag.

"Thanks for being nice to my sister, Milton," he said.

I shrugged.

He said, "Did you hear about Adam Blessing?"

I shook my head.

"Wait till you hear this," he said.

I listened. I even took one of the cigarettes he offered me and suffered through a small coughing fit, trying to inhale nonchalantly while he gave me all the details. His father worked for the Storm Taxi

Company and he had told Peter that last night he had driven this young girl to the Blessing place. He'd known Charlie wasn't there, because he'd taken Charlie to the Burlington Airport earlier in the week. He'd said the young girl was the flashy type with dyed hair and the smell of whiskey. She'd had a suitcase with her.

"That isn't all, either," Peter said. "This afternoon they took her out of there in an ambulance. She'd taken sleeping pills, and she was in this fire-red negligee with fur on it, and Adam was with her!"

"Wow!" I whistled.

"Yeah. Everybody's talking about it. I bet she's some whore. Do you think she's some whore?"

I shrugged and stepped on the cigarette. I went back into the gym and searched for Christine. She was dancing with Larry Brenner, who came up to her shoulder. I went up and cut in.

"Where have you *been*?" she said.

"Never mind that," I said. "I just heard something wild about Adam!"

"I heard it, too. Ty told me. When Marlon gets here I'm Marlon's date!"

"I'm Marlon's date!" I said.

"Keep your voice down," she said. "Don't dance with me and shout out that you're Marlon's date!"

"You're Adam's date," I said.

"He's spent the night with some chorus girl!" she said.

I said, "I heard it was a whiskey-drinking whore."

"A friend of his *father's*," she said sarcastically. "He said it was a *friend* of his *father's*!"

"It's a free country," I said.

"My father was right about him. We don't know anything about him!"

"You said yourself he was different."

"Keep that head away from my shoulder and back!" she said.

"It isn't easy to dance carrying your head," I said. "You should try it sometime."

"You're going to pay for the way you've acted tonight," she said.

"Excuse me," I said. "Was that your big toe with the corn on it again?"

"I *hate* you," she said through her teeth.

"Hatred is immortal," I said.

"I think you know more about everything than you're admitting."

Ty Hardin and Diane Wattley danced past us. "Hey, Mystery Man," Ty called out. "How about some birdcalls?" He was laughing very hard.

"What is that supposed to mean?" Christine asked me.

"Rumor has it that I'm Milton Merrensky," I said.

"I wouldn't be seen dead with Milton Merrensky!" Christine said.

Ty Hardin called out again, "How about some birdcalls, Milton?"

"This is humiliating!" Christine said.

I made a bad attempt at a whippoorwill's call.

"Stop it!" Christine said.

Then Peter Pepper tapped me on the shoulder. "One good turn deserves another," he said. "May I have this dance with Christine?"

I headed immediately for the phone booths in the hall outside the gym. I decided to call the Storm hospital and see if I could reach Adam. If Adam was like a stranger to me since I'd overheard the conversation between my mother and my aunt, Adam's father didn't seem so unknown. I had seen him on television, and I had read about him in the gossip columns. If I were to make a guess who would be more likely to be friends with a flashy blonde smelling of whiskey, Adam or his father, I would choose the latter. I believed Adam, if no one else in Storm would. I was looking up the number of the hospital when two husky policemen, accompanied by Mr. Baird, headed down the hall . . . and then Ella Early yanked open the door of the phone booth.

"Wait!" she called to Mr. Baird. "Wait! He's right in here. I told you it couldn't be Adam Blessing trying to sneak in—he's right here!"

She pulled me out of the phone booth. "Adam, tell Mr. Baird who you are, for heaven's sake! There's a rumor you've just broken in through the equipment room!"

Mr. Baird had stopped in his tracks. He said to the police, "Bring the boy down in the equipment room up here." Then he turned to me. "Adam, is that you?"

"It's him," Ella Early said. "I spoke to him earlier."

"Then speak up, Adam!"

I sagged against the phone booth and stared at Mr. Baird through the holes in my sweater.

"You have a lot of explaining to do, Adam," he said. "Come to my office."

"It wasn't him involved in any of this," Ella Early said.

"You stay out of this, Ella," said Mr. Baird. "You don't know the half of this."

"I know the gossip," she said, "I'm not deaf yet. Adam," she said, trying to help me move by gently taking my arm, "tell him you've been here all evening. They say you've been at the hospital with some . . . some *hoyden* who swallowed pills."

"Come to my office, Adam," said Mr. Baird.

I was watching what was headed toward us from way down at the other end of the corridor. It was Adam. There was a policeman on either side of him. He was carrying a fur coat and a blonde wig. He had obviously tried to sneak in through the equipment room, leave the coat and wig there, and then somehow signal me to change clothes with him.

There was a crowd beginning to collect in the hall.

"You have nothing to worry about," Ella Early

said to me gently, "if you just tell the truth."

I hugged Sir Walter Raleigh's head close to my heart.

"Adam?" Ella Early persisted.

Romeo Hardin spoke up from the crowd. "That's not Adam, Miss Early, there's Adam!" He stood there grinning with satisfaction as Adam approached, with both policemen holding him firmly now, as though he were an escaped convict.

Ty walked across to me. "Milton?" he said. "*I'm* taking Christine home. *You're* taking Diane Wattley home. Get it?"

Mystery Man made one last horrendous gesture with all his strength and power. I kicked Ty Hardin hard, so hard he let out a yelp of surprise and pain.

"What feels right is right," I said.

"You're not Milton Merrensky!" he said, dancing around on one leg. "You're a girl!"

I saw Queen Elizabeth then, her face screwed up like a small baby's face a moment before it began to wail. I tossed Sir Walter's head into the phone booth, and I unfastened my long cloak.

Christine let loose, orchestrating the hysteria which was fast filling the school corridor.

"Blow your nose on this," I said, dropping my cloak over her head as I passed her.

Then I joined the death procession to Mr. Baird's office.

From the Journal of A.

I spent Friday night at Mr. Baird's house, and Saturday morning we drove Electric Socket to the Burlington Airport. Later in the day I went back to my grandfather's house to pack. It was my first chance to call Christine. She answered the phone herself, and I said, "This is me. Adam. There's bad news."

"Everyone's heard and read the news by now," she said. "By now you're almost as well known as your father."

"I don't mean that news," I said. "I mean the news that I've been expelled."

"And everyone's seen your picture with that person," she said, ignoring what I'd just told her.

She was talking about the picture of Electric Socket leaving the hospital on my arm. Mr. Baird had ducked out of camera range. The picture was in the early edition of *The Evening Star* with the caption:

Son Keeps Famous Father's Flame Going

"I feel sorry for her," I told Christine.

"I feel sorry for *you*, Adam."

"Oh, I'll get into another school."

"I don't mean that, specifically. I mean everything in general. I mean about who your father is. It really makes me appreciate my own sweet, uncomplicated father."

"My father has to handle a lot," I said. "He's always under a lot of pressure." I hadn't been able to reach my father. He was out of the country on special assignment. (I wondered what important meeting they'd call him out of to give him the news, or if the reporters would spring it on him as he was rushing to his limousine.) I'd talked to Billie Kay and my grandfather in California. They'd wired money for me to join them.

"And I really appreciate my own normal homelife now," Christine continued.

"Well, I'm glad of that. I'm glad you're not mad."

"There's nothing for me to be mad at. I'm just sorry for you."

"Don't be sorry for me," I said. "I'm not that bad off."

"I can't help being sorry for you. I could cry when I think about you, Adam."

"Listen," I said, "not everyone would be happy having a sweet uncomplicated father and a normal homelife. Did you ever think of that? Maybe I like being his son, did you ever think of that?"

"Then how come you didn't admit whose son you are?"

"What?"

"How come you pretended to be someone else if you're so happy being his son?"

"I didn't say I was happy being his son," I said. "I just said not everyone would be happy having a sweet, uncomplicated father." I was thinking of something Electric Socket told me just before she boarded the plane to go back to Hollywood. She said, "Even though things didn't work out between your father and me, Adam, I wouldn't have missed knowing him for the world. He's not an ordinary man, honey; he's not your average Tom, Dick or Harry. You can't expect your dad to act in an ordinary, average way."

I told Christine, "Not everyone is an ordinary, average man."

"I'll take *my* father any day," she said.

"Why don't we leave our fathers out of the discussion?" I said, because I hadn't called her up to talk about or defend my father, and for some reason

I could feel myself becoming really steamed when she said she pitied me because I was his son.

"That's impossible—to leave our fathers out of the discussion," she said, "under the circumstances."

"I don't want to go on and on about it," I said. "Will I see you before I go?"

"I can't."

"Your father?"

"I've promised him," she said. "But you can write, Adam. He doesn't care if we write."

"He's all heart," I said.

She said, "Adam, he's a *father*—you don't understand! He's looking out for me like a father does."

"Yes," I said. "Well, you're his major responsibility. I mean, some people are just fathers . . . or daughters . . . or sons . . . and that's it." I was thinking of myself, not just Dr. Cutler. So far in my life all I'd been was someone's son, even when I was so busy pretending I wasn't his son. I seemed to have had just one role in life: son of.

Christine said, "I wouldn't want my father to be any way but the way he is."

I suppose we could have gone on for hours comparing our fathers. I felt like asking Christine just what the hell her sweet, uncomplicated father had ever been called on to do in his life but worm people's dogs, spay their cats and prescribe remedies for constipation and diarrhea in four-legged creatures.

212

I mean, *my* father had been chosen to address the United Nations, sat at dinner with heads of state, and slept under the same roof with presidents, kings and foreign ministers!

But it would only have sounded like sour grapes, and I didn't feel bitter or argumentative. Instead, I felt like doing a lot of thinking about my old man, which would take a long time, because he was so much more than just my old man.

I said, "I can't think of anything else to say, Christine."

"I understand. Write to me, Adam."

"Okay," I said, because you can't answer "What about?" when someone says "Write to me." But what would I have written about to Christine? We never really even knew each other.

"Good-bye, Adam."

She said it, so I didn't have to.

Notes for a Novel by B.B.B.

"Brenda Belle?" he said, "This is me. Adam. I spent the night at Mr. Baird's."

"What's his house like?" I said. "Has his wife really got a wart on the tip of her nose?"

"His house is all right," he said. "Yes, she really has a wart on the end of her nose. . . . I'm sorry you were put on probation, Brenda Belle. *I've* been expelled."

"I hate him!" I said. "A lot!"

"He really feels badly," he said. "He says he has to do it, for the sake of the school . . . and the Board of Directors."

"For the sake of the *school*!" I shouted. "The school ought to be thankful someone like your father would let you throw spitballs at his blackboards!

What is that school ever going to be known for? Nobody important ever went to that school! That school hasn't graduated anybody but a bunch of Joe Schmucks and Nancy Nowheres! That is a real lemon high school!"

Adam said, "Well anyway, I'll be heading out to the coast tonight to join my grandfather."

"Winging it to the coast, huh?" I laughed to keep from crying.

"Yeah," he chuckled.

"That was a neat picture of you and Electric Socket," I said. "My mother said she took those pills for a publicity stunt, to get her name in all the papers."

"That's not true," Adam said. "She really fell for my father."

"He's too restless a man to settle down with one woman, my aunt says."

"I guess so," Adam said.

"My aunt says a man like your father has too much on his mind to think seriously about romance."

"He's not your ordinary, average man," Adam said.

"I'm being punished," I said, "for being put on probation. I wish I could see you before you go."

Adam could probably tell from the breaks in my voice that I was on the verge of bawling. He said, "Don't feel bad, Brenda Belle. We'll write. Maybe you'll come out to the coast to visit me."

"My aunt would like your father's autograph," I said. It was a lie. I wanted it.

"I'll send her an autographed photograph," Adam said.

"Tell him to write on it 'For Brenda Belle Blossom.'"

Adam laughed. He said, "I'm not going to say good-bye."

"You don't think *I* am?" I said.

So we both hung up without saying it.

From the Journal of A.

CHUCK FROM VERMONT'S

ICE CREAM BOAT
featuring
44 Boat Flavors
New England Baked Beans
Storm Chili
Free Advice on Animal Care
and

BILLIE KAY CASE OF SCREEN FAME
BEHIND THE SCOOPER-DOOPER

The franchise people were by again last night to chew out my grandfather for deviating from the tested formula for a successful Ice Cream Boat. My grandfather and Billie Kay operate the 98th branch, and it is the only one pushing things besides ice cream. Even though my grandfather is doing a tremendous business, the franchise people are against any innovations which do not originate in the home office.

"What did you tell them?" Billie Kay asked. We were all having breakfast on Billie Kay's patio. It was warm this morning, a typical California day in May, slightly smoggy, but the sun was out. The apartment my grandfather and I rent from Billie Kay overlooks the patio and her backyard, filled with orange and avocado trees and Janice's catnip patch.

My grandfather took a swallow from his can of beer (he's given up spritzers and ascots, and he's back to falling asleep nights with all his clothes on). He said, "I told them I'd attend to it." He was munching on a piece of bacon and making a new sign: **New England Clam Chowder, 40¢ A Bowl!** "But I didn't tell them *when*," he snorted.

Janice was trying to avoid Billie Kay, who was trying to catch her so she could pet her and play her idea of a tickle game with the cat. Janice always made it over the garden wall before Billie Kay could grab her collar.

"They'll catch up with us one day," said Billie Kay.

"So will the undertaker and the gravedigger," said

my grandfather. "I have no past and no future, just today. I intend to enjoy today!"

"That reminds me of something from Christopher Fry's *The Dark Is Light Enough*," said Billie Kay. "It goes: 'If we could make each morning with no memory Of living before we went to sleep, we might Arrive at a faultless day. . . .'"

"Speaking of fry," said my grandfather, "we ought to think about adding fish fries."

"Who's going to buy ice cream in a place smelling of fish?" I said. I was sitting there finishing a plate of scrambled eggs and trying to read a letter from Brenda Belle.

"He's got a point, Charlie," Billie Kay said.

"I'm not taking the advice of anyone who isn't even bothering to finish high school," my grandfather answered.

It was another nudge stemming from my unwillingness to make up my mind whether or not I'd enroll in summer school out here. I'd have to, if I wanted to enter junior year in Hollywood High. We'd talked about it a lot: the idea of me working in the Boat and attending high school. My grandfather was always making cracks about living with a dummy who'd probably have to go to body-fender repair school one day to learn a trade.

I wasn't in the mood to argue the point this morning, or go into the matter at any length. I read Brenda

Belle's letter with a mixture of curiosity and removal. I was still close enough to Storm to be interested in the gossip, but in another way I was light-years from that period in my life.

I had thought, when I first moved in with my grandfather out here, that I would worm from him the exact truth concerning my father and mother, and my mother's accident. There are still many pieces to the puzzle which I haven't fit into place. I know that my mother didn't love him when she married him, that having me didn't make her love him any more, and that she ultimately ran off and left me with him. I know that she was killed in the automobile accident on her way out of Storm. . . . Did my grandfather kick her out when she showed up there? . . . Was she leaving Storm because my father was on his way to bring her back? They are unanswered questions, and the few efforts I made at posing them brought defeated sighs from my grandfather, and painful "I don't want to talk about it" responses.

Maybe Christopher Fry is right: We should wake each morning with no memory of living before we went to sleep; maybe it is just best to get on with things—I don't know. I do know that if the answers to my existence are rooted in my mother's existence, then hers are rooted in my grandfather's and his are rooted in my great-grandfather's, on and on . . . on and on. And I would have to trace back the whole history on my father's side . . . and when I was ancient and awaiting the undertaker and the gravedigger, I might finally have all the answers and the exact truth.

But I have my own life to live, and I want to start. I have people to meet who will have nothing to do with my father or my mother, and places to see where things will happen solely to me.

This morning I thought all this through again, and I thought a lot about my father. I see him in another, softer light . . . not because he's become any softer (he hasn't), but because I appreciate now why he never drops his guard, or trusts, or lets himself become too seriously involved with anyone. . . . It is possible that all the hurt has made him so good at what he does; it is equally possible that such a man is only good at what he does, and not good at all at the things most men do easily. The only thing I'm really sure about where my father is concerned is that he's different. Special, you might say. An extraordinary man.

This afternoon when my father telephoned, I was ready for him. He was calling from Paris. He's going to be there awhile, then on to Russia, India and China. He's dating a chanteuse named Huguette. ("Not You-get, A.J.," he told me when I talked with him last week. "If you pronounce her name You-get, you get nothing—ha-ha! It's *Oo*-get.")

"Have you decided whether you want to join me this summer, A.J.?"

"Yes."

"Well for God's sake, out with it!" he barked. "I'm not in Santa Monica."

"I'm coming," I said.

My father isn't big in the world of elated responses. Maybe the announcement that I am joining him didn't leave him particularly elated. No reason why it should. It's enough that he asked me.

"I'll make arrangements," he said.

"I'll be ready to leave June first."

"Don't pack a lot of stuff. We'll travel light."

"That suits me fine," I said.

One day, no doubt, I will find myself enrolled in yet another school. It might even *be* a body-fender repair school, as my grandfather threatens—there's just no telling. In the meantime, I am not going to sweat it.

We'll travel light—I like that. I'm not ready for anything heavy. I want to start out slow and easy while I get used to a few things . . . like all the advantages of being the son of someone famous. That's just a part of being me. But not the biggest part. I know that now.

Notes for a Novel by B.B.B.

Some of you would probably imagine that a happy ending to my story would be an announcement that my voice had risen several pitches and that I no longer have any fuzz on my upper lip.

As my Aunt Faith would say, *that* is an untruth.

But there are those among you, I know, who will perceive the fact that I am not ending on an unhappy note, when I tell you that I'll be singing alto-bordering-on-bass in the Storm High graduation choir, and that I am now into celebrating my fuzz, wherever it appears: lip, underarms, legs. I have gone natural.

"Brenda Belle," my mother tells me, "you should spend a little more time on your grooming, particularly if you plan to visit Adam out in California this summer." My mother is a big hit at our local beauty parlor, where she sits under the drier holding forth on the subject of Adam and his father. She enlarges on things as she goes along, though her natural survival instinct keeps her from involving Dr. Cutler in any way. The past improves, they say . . . and her opinion of Adam is now at its highest point since she and Aunt Faith first viewed Adam as "that poor kid living down there with old Charlie."

"Mother," I tell her, "I'm not sure Hollywood is my style right now. I may not go out there. Tinsel Town is not a very natural place."

"Neither is Hogg's Swamp a very natural place for a young girl to spend her time with a boy," my mother answers.

"With a boy like Milton Merrensky, it *is*," I reply.

"What do you *do* down there?" she asks, and never tires of asking.

"We practice birdcalls, for one thing," I tell her. "Do you want to hear a whippoorwill?"

"Not *again*, Brenda Belle! Please!"

I don't blame her. I am awful at whippoorwills, I have discovered. But I can do a mean male chaffinch, and a dandy tooth-billed bowerbird.

"Do Christine Cutler and Peter Pepper ever go to Hogg's Swamp?" my mother asks.

"Never!"

"Or Ty Hardin and Diane Wattley?"

"They're too busy with lovers' quarrels."

"Marlon Fredenberg and Marilyn Pepper?"

"They never leave the back seat of his old Chevy."

"Oh dear," my mother moans softly to herself, "oh dear, oh dear," a familiar exclamation from my mother these days, about a lot of things, from the fact I refuse to throw out the smelly sweet potato plant I rescued from Dr. Blessing's house (I am inventing a charcoal filter to eliminate the odor) to the fact that his house was sold to a religious commune of young people called "Christ's Stormtroopers."

I have learned a lot of things since Adam first appeared in Storm. Most of them I keep to myself, like the true story of Christine's father and Adam's mother. I see him around Storm, sometimes, and seeing him gives me a new calm. If that docile little man with a bald head and spectacles can star in a romantic drama which anyone would care to still whisper about years hence, then there is no trick to this romance business. For all I ever knew about people before all this happened, there were duels fought at dawn over Ella Early, and Rufus Kerin fathered famous princes in secret.

The thing is, you just can't tell about people, even when you think you know everything there is to know about them.

Take Milton Merrensky, for example. He isn't shy at all. He just doesn't have a lot to say, because very few people discuss the things that interest him. How many people in Storm, Vermont, even care that courtship feeding is a feature of the precopulatory behavior of most finches, or that turkeys blush? How many people in the whole world can imitate the nesting call of the violet-eared waxbill? Milton Merrensky can.

I am beginning to see past The Pillars and Corps Drugs, and all the tacky and familiar facades of Storm, to other worlds within my own world, where minute creatures thrive, and plant life I had never known existed grows and changes with the season. . . . I see, too, the world beyond my world, Australia, for example, where megapodes build mounds ten feet high around their egg chambers; and the forests of Central America, where the marbled wood quails sing duets.

"Milton Merrensky!" my mother sighs. "*I* wouldn't be interested in him for a boyfriend."

"He wouldn't be interested in you for a girlfriend, either," I answer, though Milton has often remarked favorably on my mother's striking resemblance to a great crested grebe, known for its violent headshaking in courtship ceremonies.

"Brenda Belle," my mother says, "I'm not criticizing you. But I have this feeling, this very definite feeling that you are slipping away from the crowd— that you are losing interest in the things other girls in Storm care about."

This time I think my mother's right.